SNOWED IN WITH DEATH

HOLLY WINTER MYSTERIES

RUBY LOREN

BRITISH AUTHOR

Please note, this book is written in British English and contains British spellings.

BOOKS IN THE SERIES

SNOWED IN WITH DEATH

THE DUNCE DETECTIVE

Holly frowned at the first flurry of snow when it splattered wetly on her windscreen. Her wipers soon cleared her vision of the road again, but the white stuff was definitely here to stay.

She bit her lip and wondered if she'd make it to Horn Hill House before the road became impassable. There'd been a weather warning for snow when she'd left her cottage in Little Wemley (a village in deepest, darkest Surrey) early that morning. She'd driven away sooner than she'd originally planned, but the bad weather had also been annoyingly punctual.

"A bit of snow won't keep me away," she muttered under her breath. Even if volcanoes popped up like pimples, and frogs started raining down from the sky, she was certain she'd still figure out how to get to Horn Hill House. The event she was on her way to attend was the chance of a lifetime. Nothing would persuade her to miss it. She could only hope that the other esteemed guests attending the convention were just as committed.

The competition win had been a complete surprise.

Even the most talented detective in the world couldn't predict blind luck. Holly had been thrilled when she'd received the email inviting her to the annual meeting of the greatest private detectives in Britain. During her time off - between occasional small-time mystery cases and her evening work as a professional lounge pianist - she was a coffee break 'comper'. This particular competition win had seemed like fate.

It's going to be amazing finding out what it's like working as a real private detective! she thought, turning down a narrow country lane and swerving to avoid a wandering sheep that had momentarily looked unnervingly like a walking snowman.

Holly had already investigated her fair share of mysteries.

She'd recently traced and recovered her next door neighbour's stolen dog. Her discovery had resulted in the prosecution of a group of exceedingly nasty human beings who'd been organising dog-baiting events. Holly had been incredibly relieved that she'd managed to solve the mystery and save 'Smosage' the sausage dog, before he'd been thrown into the ring as bait.

Well... sort of relieved.

The tiny dog had shown his gratitude by latching onto her ankle and refusing to let go when she'd tried to put him in her car. He'd topped off his thank you by being sick all over the upholstery.

Still... her neighbour Doris had been suitably grateful for his return, and Holly would never admit that she'd been very tempted to keep on driving when the silly dog had spotted a rabbit by the side of the road and launched himself through her unwisely open window. They'd been bombing along a dual carriageway at the time.

There'd also been the case of the mayor's missing chain. The Little Wemley mayor's chain was something rather special. It was an antique from the Victorian period and - for no apparent reason other than the decadence of whomever must have been the mayor at the time - it was encrusted with rubies.

In truth, it was rather unsurprising that somebody stole it.

It hadn't even been the first time that the chain was 'borrowed without permission'. Holly had been called upon to solve the mystery twice before.

In the case of the first disappearance, it had transpired that the mayor had only mislaid the chain. The missing village heirloom had turned up a few days later in a drawer. The second time, the mayor forgot that he'd asked his secretary to arrange for the chain to be cleaned.

On the third occasion the chain disappeared, it really had been stolen. Holly had searched for clues and managed to trace the thief's whereabouts to the local pub, where she'd found him loudly boasting about the success of his theft. It wasn't really a case worthy of Sherlock Holmes, but it had got her name in the paper again.

Holly had definitely started to build a reputation for solving mysteries. Or, if you asked her arch-enemy - sorry - *sister*, Annabelle: 'sticking her nose into other people's business'.

Holly brushed a stray strand of her dark brown fringe out of her eyes and vaguely wondered what to get Annabelle for Christmas. She couldn't remember if she'd already given her a lump of coal...

The strand of hair fell back down and tangled with her eyelashes. Holly huffed a breath out, blowing it skywards. She knew she should have had a haircut before leaving for Scotland, but there hadn't been time. Her schedule in the run-up to Christmas was always packed - as was her pianist's brain with every Christmas song ever written. There hadn't been time for a trim.

She frowned at herself in the rearview mirror, wondering if it was worth risking a quick snip with the nail scissors she'd packed in her suitcase. The last time she'd cut her own fringe, she'd ended up with a patch of stubby hair sticking straight up above her forehead, but then, she had only been five-years-old at the time. Haircutting ability was something you naturally developed with age... right?

Her preoccupation with her infuriating fringe almost made her miss the turning. The signpost was already half-crusted with fresh snowfall. It was only some extra sense that turned her gaze and revealed the words: 'orn Hill Hou' - the other letters already concealed by feathery flakes.

She slammed the brakes on and then remembered how important it was to not do anything sudden (like slamming the brakes on) in icy weather. "Fudgecicles!" she said (or at least, something that *sounded* similar) when her car slid around the bend and gently bumped against a hedge. The branches immediately shed their full-load of snow onto her roof.

Holly twitched her head from side to side and was relieved to discover that no one had witnessed her little bump. She didn't want to appear anything less than competent when she met her professional idols. She'd already researched each of the seven detectives who were attending their annual convention at the house. She'd even made a fact file. They were so well-known it had been easy to read up on all of their greatest cases. She only hoped that they might see some spark of the same potential in her...

"This has to be it..." she muttered under her breath when she turned a corner on the long driveway. The imposing outline of Horn Hill House loomed over the bleak landscape, silhouetted on the brow of a hill against the curiously orange sky.

Holly drove onwards, her wipers furiously swiping the snow away. Every time her car's wheels skidded a little on the settling snow, her heart jumped in her chest. She hoped that the seven detectives had shared the same foresight and had chosen to arrive early. It didn't seem likely that the drive up to Horn Hill House would be passable for much longer.

Please don't let me be the only one here! she suddenly thought and wondered (in a slight panic) what would happen if she was stuck in the middle of nowhere, without any way of getting into the house? Visions of her having to break-in popped into her head. She crossed her fingers on the wheel. It wouldn't come to that.

She drove into the gravelled car park, her wheels making squeaking noises against the snow. Six cars were already parked. Holly suddenly wondered if she was late after all... before realising that the detectives were one step ahead of her. She shook her head in amazement and felt a thrill of uncertainty. Holly suspected that she was already out of her league, and she hadn't even met the seven, yet!

The snow blew straight into her face when she opened the car door and stepped out into the arctic landscape. With an almost audible 'ping', Holly's fringe sensed the cold weather and curled up of its own accord. She swore and desperately patted the rest of her now-maniacal hairdo.

So much for first impressions.

Holly felt a swirl of emotion twist in her gut when she looked at the bright lights that shone from within Horn Hill House. In the midst of the snowstorm it should have been an inviting image, but her hands shook with the same stage-fright she always suffered from whenever she played the piano at big events.

These detectives were already on their way to becoming

legends. She'd found a lost dog and a chain - stolen by a man who was more 'village idiot' than 'master-criminal'. Why would any of them give her the time of day?

A little voice in her head whispered that even the greats had to start somewhere... She didn't even have any serious aspirations to be a professional, right? She was perfectly happy solving mysteries in her spare time and being a professional pianist by night.

The little voice inside her head laughed at her transparent attempt to convince herself that she lacked ambition. Holly pretended not to hear it. She also ignored the stab of unease that grew in the pit of her stomach - putting it down to a fresh attack of nerves.

But it wasn't just a bad case of the jitters. It was a ghostly premonition of a terrible future that was lying in wait within Horn Hill House.

The next twenty-four hours would be a deadly dance with death.

And not everyone was going to make it out alive.

LET THE GAMES BEGIN

Six heads turned her way when she walked into the living room.

The front door had been open a crack, so Holly had let herself in. She'd patted her hair down as best as she could, being simultaneously grateful and regretful that there'd been no mirror in which to check her reflection. She wasn't particularly vain, choosing to dress in clothes that suited her, rather than the latest fashions. She also never did anything fancy with her hair and makeup; but extreme weather conditions tended to transform her from Little-Miss-Normal into the swamp beast from the black lagoon. She hoped that the detectives would use their famed powers of deduction to deduce that she didn't always look this terrible.

The smile jumped onto her face a couple of seconds too late when she realised they were all staring, waiting for her to say something. "Hi, I'm Holly," she supplied, pleased that her voice sounded pretty level. "You must be the detectives. Although, there are only six of you…" She'd looked around and had picked up on the obvious.

"Ah, yes… Holly Winter - our lucky competition winner. I'm glad you made it through the bad weather." A woman clutching a large and ornate organiser got to her feet and flashed Holly the brightest smile she'd seen in a long time. Pale-pink stained lips, a hint of blusher, and natural honey blonde hair - that seemed unfairly neat and tidy - completed the other woman's perfect first impression.

"You're not one of the detectives," Holly said and then bit her tongue. She was letting her mouth run away with her!

Fortunately, the woman didn't mind. She even laughed. The high, tinkling sound would have been more appropriate coming from a fairy.

"That's right. I'm not! Much like you, I'm a fan of these legendary private detectives' work. Every year, it's my job to select a venue and organise this event. This year, it was a bit of a challenge," she added, looking thoughtful for a moment. She shook her head, before sliding a pair of designer glasses up her nose and glancing down at her organiser. "I'm afraid that one of our number called me early this morning to let me know that he couldn't make it, due to fears about the weather." The woman looked side-ways out of the window. "Regretfully, I may have hinted that he was being a little overcautious, but looking out there now… he had a point." The smile faded for a second, before it was renewed with an even more luminous one. Holly wondered if she'd be willing to part with the number for her dentist. "Still! We'll have a cosy time up here together, swapping exciting stories about what's happened during the past year."

Holly caught the two female detectives glancing at one another and flicking their gaze upwards. She got the message - this organiser was trivialising all of the work and risk they put into their jobs and their life. However, she also observed that the moment was over in a second. Some people were just sweet and fluffy by nature. These detectives bore their organiser no ill will. It was clearly just her way.

"Oh, how could I?!" the bubbly blonde exclaimed, looking so horrified Holly wondered what dreadful thing she'd done. "I haven't introduced you to anyone! My name's Miranda Louis. As I said when I was chattering away back then, I'm the event organiser. This gentleman is Jack Dewfall." She pointed to the man seated to her left. He was in his early thirties and sported an army regulation hair cut. His physique, however, was not regulation. He'd developed a strange soft paunch that seemed premature in relation to his age. Being familiar with his cases, Holly was a little surprised by his personal appearance - but she suspected it was a classic reminder that appearances are often deceptive.

"Next to him is Lydia Burns." One of the two other women present - a well-kept lady in her forties, with an enviable sheet of dark hair and perfectly applied red lipstick - inclined her head.

"You've probably heard about her cases," Miranda carried on. Holly nodded in what she hoped was a non-committal manner. She knew them all, but after Miranda's admission to also being a fan, and the almost-eye rolling that had passed between two of the detectives, she'd decided to keep that information close to her chest.

"And then we have Pete Black…"

"Adventurer, detective, and everyday hero at your service," the man finished with a slanting grin and a wink at Holly. His flashy blonde hair was decisively parted in a style reminiscent of a bygone era.

The sound of a hastily-stifled cough came from the other side of the table. Pete narrowed his eyes and shot daggers in the direction of the remaining female detective. She pretended not to notice his gaze and made a big deal of examining her deep-green, manicured nails.

"And this is Emma White," Miranda said with false brightness.

Holly could almost touch the building tension.

Emma smiled at Holly - the most genuine smile she'd seen so far. Holly couldn't help but like the other woman, who was in her late twenties - close to Holly's own age. She and Pete were the youngest detectives there, but they had both already achieved so much during their careers.

"Don't worry, I'll skip the entirely unnecessary introduction where I try to jump straight into your pants," Emma said airily, studiously ignoring the fist-clenching and head-shaking that took place on the opposite side of the table.

Holly risked a little smile back, privately wondering what had happened to make relations so frigid between the pair. She supposed it was the obvious, given Emma's larger than life dyed auburn hair, natural prettiness, and fast tongue. Team that with Pete's good looks and arrogance, and you had a perfect recipe for disaster.

"Anyway, this is Lawrence Richards," Miranda finished, visibly pleased to have completed all of the introductions without any physical fights breaking out.

The front door banged and juddered as it was thrown open, pushed by the howling wind. Heads turned again when a new visitor entered the room.

"Sorry I'm late. Can you believe this weather? I did not see it coming. I set out this morning in shorts and a t-shirt," the new arrival said with an easy grin.

All around the table, the detectives muttered their derision at this inexcusable lack of foresight, as the man - who could only be Rob Frost - sauntered inside. Holly felt a rush of exhilaration when she realised - with an odd kind of relief - that he wasn't the one who'd cancelled his invitation.

She was in the presence of the man who had solved every single unsolved robbery case he'd turned his hand to. Gold bullion, hidden for decades, had been dug up by him, and bounty worth millions was recovered and returned - no matter how smart the thieves had been. Rob was a personal favourite of Holly's. She even privately thought that his off-the-wall cases and style of investigation could easily be turned into their own book or TV series.

"Wow, Tom... you look different. But hey, I'm not judging," Rob said, grinning at Holly and raising his hands in mock defence.

Miranda cleared her throat and belatedly introduced Holly, who was already blushing under Rob's scrutiny.

She did the only thing she could think of doing and scrutinised him right back.

Rob was in his mid-thirties, and would definitely have looked more at home on an assault course than the army specialist, Jack. He was probably a little over six-foot-three tall, with broad shoulders and an easy way of standing that let you know he was completely at ease with himself. His hair was dark and trimmed close at the sides with some longer growth on the top. The only thing that really made him stand out as a detective was his dark eyes that seemed to be taking in a hundred observations to every one that Holly made. She felt like she may as well be standing naked in front of him.

The blush rose in her cheeks again and she finally broke eye contact - just catching a glimpse of the small smile that danced on Rob's lips, before he spun a chair around and plonked himself down on it.

"So, what's been happening guys? I want the real stories this time, not all of that PR spin your agents sold to the papers. Lydia, did it really take you three whole months to figure out that it was poisoned lipstick that killed all those supermodels, or were you just playing dumb to claim more on your expenses? Come on, you can tell me." He winked at the other detective.

Lydia sat back in her chair and made a huffing sound that let them all know this kind of taunting was beneath her.

Her superior silence didn't last for long. "You'd understand the magnitude of the challenge if you saw just how much gear those girls use to get ready!" she protested.

Rob's eyebrows shot up. "You're telling me they were all on drugs as well? Surely that was the first thing you told them to avoid?" He shook his head in amused disapproval.

Lydia reached a hand up - as if to tear her own hair out - but then thought better of it.

Rob just grinned. "Only kidding, Lyds. I wouldn't have cracked it that much faster than you. I reckon it would have taken me at least a week," he said, his tone serious.

Across the table, Pete spluttered out a laugh. "I could have done it in days…" he claimed, making Emma snort.

"I doubt you'd have ever solved it. You'd be too busy chasing tail to catch the killer," she sniped.

Holly noticed Miranda wincing. Confrontation was clearly something she hated.

"Let the games begin." Rob grinned, spreading his hands wide.

"How about we kick off the story telling? That way, everyone can have their say," Miranda suggested, like she was talking to a group of unruly school-children.

To Holly's surprise, the tension immediately diffused and the detectives mumbled their agreement. Miranda's overly sweet, patronising way of speaking to them, strangely had the desired effect on the highly-strung detectives.

"By the way… who drove into the hedge on the way in here? I thought all of you super-sleuths would have seen a little corner coming," Rob said, laughing at his own joke.

Holly subtly covered her face with her hand.

Great.

So, this was what it was like spending time with people who noticed every single detail. She had a feeling this weekend was going to keep her on her toes.

If she'd known what was waiting just around the corner, she'd probably have wished herself at a convention for bankers instead of detectives.

Then again... even death may be more preferable than that.

"Okay, let's do a little show-and-tell, shall we?" Miranda suggested, still in primary school teacher mode. After everything she'd heard during the last five minutes, Holly understood why. "Rob, you were the last in, so how about you go first?" Miranda asked, flashing the male detective a beautiful smile.

Holly's heart sank to the floor. She frowned and ignored the unwelcome sensation.

Rob sat back and ruffled his hair, somehow contriving to make it look even more attractive. "Well, I don't like to brag... but I've beaten you all again. I think it's only right that everyone else goes first." He grinned around the room.

Holly heard a couple of grumbles, from which she inferred that Rob made a similar claim every year.

Rob Frost just shook his head and raised his eyes heavenwards in mock exasperation. "Now, now, Jack... no need for jealousy. I know you work with the military to prove how tough you are, but some of us don't have to compensate for anything... if you know what I mean." Rob winked at Jack, who tried very hard to act as though he was above all of this.

Fortunately for everyone's sanity, there was someone in the room who was struggling to stay silent.

TROLLEY DASH OF TERROR

"Listen up people! Once you hear about my case, you won't be laughing about murderous schoolgirls any more," Pete began.

"Why? Is your story not about murderous schoolgirls? And if not, why mention them at all?" Rob asked, looking genuinely confused.

Pete's bottom lip jutted out a little. "Technically, there were murderous schoolgirls... but the case was a lot more intricate and deadly than it might initially have appeared, given the dismal way the press reported it."

"I seem to remember reading that you were obliviously dating the leader of the crime ring. I can't believe you'd sink as low as dating a schoolgirl. Wait... actually, I can, " Emma commented.

Pete was looking sulkier by the second. "She wasn't a schoolgirl! She just employed and influenced a gang of highly-violent, armed schoolgirls," he explained. It was with an effort that he managed to summon up a halfhearted slanted smile. "What can I say? I like bad girls."

Emma mimed sticking her fingers down her throat.

"You dated the leader of the entire operation without knowing that she was the leader of the entire operation?" Jack said, disbelievingly.

Pete looked like he might be about to explode. "Well, what may have started out as one thing, soon became the key to my undercover success…" he began again, but was cut off by another loud snort from Emma.

Holly was starting to wonder if she had issues with her sinuses as well as issues with Pete.

"I read that you were still hooking up with her until the day she was arrested. For some reason, the killer schoolgirls managed to evade every sting operation the police planned. Probably because you were blabbing about it to their boss. Then, when the game was up - after the police finally caught one of the little terrors - you happened to be staying at the leader's house and managed to overpower her, just before the police arrived. For some reason, someone was stupid enough to credit you with solving the case and being a big hero." Emma pretended to look thoughtful. "Seriously, who is your publicist? They really know how to work miracles." She flashed a cruel smile in the other detective's direction.

He sighed and looked towards the ceiling. "That's not how it actually went down, but you've basically ruined the story, and I really cannot be bothered to correct you. Believe what you want, but that was a tough case, and I got to the bottom of it. No more schoolgirls wielding sharp objects," Pete said, crossing his arms and sinking down into his chair.

Emma smirked around the room, but the other detectives were all pretending to be engrossed in drinking their various beverages. The rivalry between Pete and Emma was too much for any of them to stomach, and no one wanted to pick sides.

"Seeing as you're all so quiet, I think it's time for me to tell you all about my greatest case of this year. Pete, you might get bored. It doesn't involve any schoolgirls." Emma shot a look of mock concern across the table.

Pete pretended to be removing an imaginary spot of lint from his shirt.

"The case of the Tommy Gun murders wasn't one I was initially assigned. It was just a result of me being in the right place at the right time - something which does seem to happen a lot to me," she admitted with a great deal of false modesty.

"It's because you're always sticking your nose into other people's business," Pete sniped.

Emma pretended he didn't exist. "I was doing some shopping in Hull when I heard the gunshots. Naturally, I went to see what was happening."

"While *normal* people ran the other way..." Pete muttered.

"By the time I got there, the action had finished, but the man who'd been attacked was still there, lying in a pool of blood. I was just in time to hear his final words 'Tommy Gun'. I knew then that I had a case. I had to find out the meaning of the dead man's mysterious last words. Of course, I went on to singlehandedly bring down the mafia gang who'd been extorting money from Hull's businesses for years. Although, I had no idea that I'd achieve all of that back on that fateful, tragic day..."

"I heard that you neglected to mention to the investigating officers that the dead man had spoken to you before he died. Didn't the police nearly arrest you for withholding evidence?" Pete interjected.

Emma frowned. "If they wanted the evidence, they should have been there to collect it. I'm not responsible for lazy police work. Anyway, they thanked me in the end!" she said brightly, and then frowned, forgetting where she was in her story.

"We get it. You found out 'Tommy Gun' was a guy with a

stupid name. You stuck your nose into lots of people's business and made such a big noise about the local mafia that the police had to take action, or publicly lose confidence. Jolly well done," Pete said, his arms firmly folded.

Emma smiled at him. "Thanks Pete, that means a lot coming from you."

Pete opened his mouth to argue that he had definitely not meant it, but shut it again.

Emma smirked triumphantly.

"Hey, Lawrence, I never really hear about your successes. It's only the messy, messy failures that hit the headlines. What have you been up to this year?" Rob asked.

Lawrence's eyes darted around the room for a second. "You know I can't say what I've been doing. Everything is classified information!" he squeaked, his voice thin as a reed.

Rob nodded enthusiastically. "Sure, sure... Official Secrets Act and all that jazz, but what about hypothetically? Just make something up! If they're still alive, we'll know you did a good job - and hey, just hypothetically, right? Between old friends?" he wheedled, but Lawrence's lips were zipped shut.

"There are no secrets with my cases," Lydia began, flicking her dark hair back over her shoulders. "The case of the lipstick killers was my greatest success of the past year. It all began when..." Everyone around the table exchanged looks, and Lydia faltered.

"Sorry Lyds, you should be pleased... but that case was in practically every magazine and newspaper because of the models dying. I think I know every single detail inside and out. But you looked great in all the press shots!" Emma said, surprisingly tactfully.

Lydia's smile only wobbled for a second before it lifted again. "They were quite flattering, weren't they?" she said, and everyone breathed a collective sigh of relief.

Holly had also heard about the case back when it had all taken place. Emma was right to claim that it had been impossible to avoid. The press had flocked to cover the murders of the beautiful people and had reported the crimes in glorious, technicolor detail.

"I suppose that means it's my turn," Jack said, before launching into a story so convoluted and full of military jargon that Holly barely understood a word of it. If that wasn't confusing enough, half of the information was classified, so as well as jargon to contend with, there were also large holes in the plot. By the end, all she could figure out was that Jack may have averted a bomber from attacking a local supermarket by bundling him into a trolley and pushing him down a hill - so that he exploded away from innocent civilians.

"Wow, Jack… that was killer! I won't need to read any of the Andy McNab books I brought with me now," Rob said with a smirk.

Jack scowled at him. "Your turn, Rob. How many holes have you dug yourself out of this year?" Jack asked, trying to rile the other man.

"I think what you meant to ask was 'How many holes have I dug myself into?'," Rob corrected, a stupid grin on his face.

"I'm guessing the answer is a lot of them," Emma said, her mouth twitching up at one side.

Miranda glanced down at her rose gold and sparkly diamanté watch and gave a squeak of alarm. "Sorry, Rob. You'll have to tell us over dinner. You should all go and freshen up. We'll meet back down here in fifteen minutes. Otherwise, the roast will be ruined," she said, before rushing off in the direction of the kitchen.

"What a shame. I pity you all having to wait in such suspense," Rob said, doing his best to look truly concerned.

"Don't worry, Rob. That's fifteen minutes more you can use to make up something good." Jack's smile was frosty.

"Ah well… at least I won't have to be too creative this year to wipe the floor with your trolley dash of terror." Rob shot another grin at Jack, and then swiftly exited the room before the other man could reply… or throw anything heavy at him.

THE MURDERER IN THEIR MIDST

Arriving on time was apparently not cool.

While waiting for the others to arrive, Holly had ventured into the dining room to find it was decorated ready for the evening meal. Gold, bauble-adorned wreaths hung around the room, and even the mounted head of a roaring red deer stag hadn't escaped. Tinsel was woven through its antlers. Despite the big day still being weeks away, crackers were out on the table and candles were lit. The fireplace was disappointingly empty, but the room's heat was kept in by the thick, dark-blue velvet drapes that blocked out the snow scenes.

"Do you know what the roast for dinner is yet?" Emma White called, sashaying down the staircase in a beautiful beige dress with colourful flowers splashed all over it. Holly suddenly wondered if her white mini-dress and beige tights were a little plain. She wished she'd thought to pack something in a different colour. With so much snow around, she'd probably disappear if she wasn't careful.

"I don't know. It smells like something is being deep fat fried," Holly confessed, already wondering if this was some secret test. Could all proper private detectives pinpoint what was for dinner, just by smelling the air in the hallway? Emma tilted her head and then nodded in vague agreement.

"Whatever it is, I don't know about you... but I'd take Rob Frost over dessert any day. I think he's been spending more time in the gym than on the case recently, but I am not complaining about that." She flashed a conspirator's smile at Holly, who echoed it back, weakly, wondering if it was always like this in the world of investigating. Did everyone constantly swap partners? It seemed a little incestuous. The annoying voice in her head piped up to tell her that she was just jealous. She'd felt that familiar jolt of attraction when Rob had walked into the room for the first time. Her intuition hinted that the way he'd looked at her was a sign that the impressive detective had felt it too, but her knowledge of his great deeds wouldn't allow her to believe it. There was just no way she had a chance - especially with Emma, and perhaps even Miranda, as her rivals.

Fortunately, her tirade of self pity was cut short before she could make a fool out of herself by telling Emma what a perfect couple with perfect children she and Rob would make. Lawrence strolled down the stairs, nodding his thinning head in their direction, before walking straight past them towards the kitchen. Clearly, appetite came before manners. Next down was Jack, who made brief conversation, before heading straight over to the drinks cabinet. Holly rather unkindly reflected that this affection for alcohol must be the reason for his curious physique. She swallowed the thought as soon as it appeared in her head, remembering that out of all of the detectives, this military specialist had probably seen harrowing scenes that were enough to drive anyone to drink.

"Oh, well, that's just typical," Emma muttered under her breath. Holly turned to see what she was talking about.

Lydia Burns was dressed in a floor-length gown that was so deep a shade of red, it almost looked like it had been stained with blood. Despite her more senior years, Holly knew she was currently outsmarting them all when it came to fashion. Her own white dress now seemed positively plain.

"What did I miss?" Rob appeared at the top of the stairs just behind Lydia. She couldn't help but wonder if…?

Emma tutted under her breath. Holly imagined they'd both made the same leap of inference. Perhaps there was hope for her as a detective after all!

Rob grinned some more. "Oh, you girls… you make me laugh," he said and walked down in a subtle haze of *Jean Paul Gautier* aftershave, leaving them all to wonder.

"Oh good, we're all here," Miranda said, appearing in the doorway of the kitchen. She was wearing a ridiculously ruffle-adorned, pink apron. It suited her.

"Uh, no… Pete's missing," Lawrence observed, his voice quiet, but carrying, in its thin way.

"Shall we get on before the food you've worked so hard to cook for us is ruined? I'm sure Pete just wants to draw out the moment for some extra attention," Emma said, and for the briefest of moments, her gaze rested on Holly.

"Ah, yes… well, it is ready," Miranda said, visibly torn between the compliment and the incendiary remark.

"Don't sweat it. I'll go back upstairs and drag him out of bed. He's probably fallen asleep. The man works too hard. What was his last case? I wasn't really listening earlier. Schoolgirls with steak knives, or something?" Rob shook his head, still smiling. "Tough crime, tough criminals."

"Just go and get him," Lydia said, most likely thinking back to Rob's cross-examination of her own case. *Or, perhaps she subscribes to the 'treat them mean to keep them keen' philosophy*, Holly thought.

"So, should we…" Miranda's hands fluttered over the

ludicrous flounces of her apron, as she hovered in the kitchen doorway. Holly wondered if Miranda really was the super fan she claimed to be, or if she was an events specialist who was paid - probably by the detectives themselves - to run the whole event and further bolster their egos by playing the part. She had a feeling she'd have figured out the answer by the end of the weekend.

"Oh my gosh, you cooked all this yourself?" Emma cooed when they entered the kitchen, sliding past a semi-protesting Miranda.

"Yes! Well, you know... it was nothing," the organiser said, slipping back into the room. She wasn't fast enough to conceal the flash of white wrapping that was sticking up from the bin. So, Miranda had her flaws, too!

Emma turned and raised an amused eyebrow at Holly, before they walked back into the dining room.

"Can I help you bring things through?" Holly asked, turning back.

Miranda stared at her like she had spoken a foreign language, before flapping a hand. "No, no. It's okay. There's really nothing to do," she said, before rushing off and making such a clattering sound, it made Holly wonder if their dinner had just ended up in the floor. Sometimes, it was better to not have an enquiring mind.

"I wonder where Rob is?" Lawrence asked, looking mildly concerned.

"I hope he didn't decide to tunnel his way into Pete's room," Jack said and guffawed loudly at his own joke. Holly opened her mouth to defend Rob, but then realised it was better not to join in the less-than-friendly competition and side-taking that was going on.

They were just about to give up waiting and start dishing up, when Rob reappeared. He looked a lot less cool and collected than he had done when he'd come down the stairs the first time.

"Pete's dead," he announced, his face pale. "Someone's killed him. There's a dagger in his chest and blood... lots of blood." What little colour remained in his cheeks vacated when he said the word 'blood'. A moment later, he pulled himself together. His mouth hardened into a determined thin line.

"I think we should all go up and take a look," Jack said, pushing his chair back. His drink and the food were forgotten.

"Maybe the ladies could wait here, and someone should stay with them..." Lawrence suggested, looking wistfully at his food.

Lydia rolled her eyes. "We've all seen our fair share of dead bodies, Lawrence. Even you don't have a perfect track record."

Lawrence stopped looking at his food. His light blue eyes sharpened behind his spectacles as he absorbed the insult.

"Well, I guess we're all going," Jack broke in, his eyes flicking up to the ceiling. Somewhere above them, Pete presumably lay dead with a knife in his chest.

"Is this some sort of a game, like a fake whodunnit to solve?" Holly whispered to Miranda, who looked horrified by the thought.

"Gosh, no! We would never trivialise..." She stopped talking. Holly wondered if she'd insulted the other woman, but to her surprise, Miranda's eyes were beading with tears. "Oh, this is awful. Everyone here is just so nice! How could anyone kill Pete?"

Holly opened her mouth to point out that the six detectives they were sharing the house with probably had more enemies than the rest of the population of Britain put together - not to mention their fierce inter-rivalry - but it didn't seem the right moment to shatter Miranda's odd delusion.

"Yup, he is definitely dead," Lydia commented, rather crassly, when they walked into Pete's bedroom.

Holly bit her lip hard, as she came face to face with her first ever dead body.

Pete's neatly side-parted hair was still in perfect condition. He lay on his back with his arms by his side. His expression held all of the serenity of someone still asleep, but Holly could tell from the grey pallor and the lack of a pulse jumping in his neck that this was one micro-nap Pete Black would not be waking up from.

"Single stab, straight into the heart. That's why there isn't a lot of blood," Jack commented. Holly tried not to hear the hint of admiration in his voice. This was an efficient kill. Also, how was this classed as being 'not a lot of blood'? She supposed the walls hadn't been redecorated, but she shared Rob's opinion rather than Jack's.

All of the visitors in the room grew silent. They stared at Pete's body for such a long time that the tension climbed to a point where Holly was half-expecting the corpse to jump up and scream at them.

"Is anyone else staying here at the house, Miranda?" Lawrence finally asked, in his usual quiet way.

Miranda quickly shook her head, her eyes determinedly fixed on the light fixture at the centre of the room.

"So... it's one of us. One of us killed Pete Black," Rob concluded, sounding horrifyingly intrigued by the idea. "We have a murderer in our midst."

DINING WITH DEATH

"I suppose now wouldn't be the time to mention my record-breaking feat of solving a case in five minutes and putting myself forward for the role of lead detective on this case?" Rob asked, looking around at the ashen faces. "No, probably not the time. Maybe after coffee and mints," he concluded.

"We've got to call for help. The police will come," Holly said.

Everyone stared at her like calling the police was a completely alien concept.

"Oh yes... the police," Lydia conceded.

There was some collective eye-narrowing.

"It is the law!" Holly persisted. There was finally some grudging agreement, although, she heard a few 'wouldn't waste my time' mutterings. They walked down the hall as a group, collectively deciding not to loiter in the room where the smell of death lingered.

"Right... here we go," Holly said, feeling a sense of trepidation, as she dialled 999.

She'd never been in an emergency before, but this was a

real-life situation, wasn't it? Someone was actually dead. She blinked a few times and wished her head would clear. How could anyone think straight after seeing something like that? It was one thing reading about violent murders in a novel, but quite another in real life. Half of her still wanted to believe that this was all part of the event - a false death set up to challenge the other detectives. Unfortunately, she knew that Pete Black was no actor. He was a genuine private detective, whose short career had just come to a brutal - and very final - end.

"Er, do they usually take so long to answer?" Holly asked, feeling stupidly unprepared for this. The phone was making a noise, but she wasn't sure if it was ringing or not.

Lydia seized the handset and listened. "Dead. Whoever did this has also cut our lines of communication."

They all pulled out their mobile phones and berated the evil genius behind the absence of cell service, until Jack pointed out that it was probably their fault for picking such a rural Scottish location for their meet up. The phone lines being down could also be explained by the snow.

"This is probably all the work of someone who had an axe to grind with Pete. Someone who's been unusually lost for words since Rob came down and told us he was dead," Jack said.

Everyone turned to look at Emma, who didn't even have the good-grace to blush. "Oh, come on! I'm the last person who'd kill him. Seriously, when is it ever the obvious suspect who actually committed the crime?" she bit back, folding her arms.

"Well, statistically..." Lawrence began, but Emma carried on speaking.

"Pete and I had a love-hate relationship, sure. But if I'd killed that smarmy, cheating, good for nothing, I wouldn't have stabbed him. I would have planned something a lot nastier. He'd have known all about it, and exactly who had done it to him, when he finally got what he deserved." She looked around brightly.

"Okay, great!" Rob said, looking nowhere near as perturbed as Holly felt. "That sounds perfectly reasonable to me. Does anyone else have questions? No? Well, how about we all go down and have some dinner? We're all together, so the killer probably won't strike again. We've all seen those bad horror movies. If we stay together, then we live. Or, hey! Look on the bright side! If someone else gets murdered, it will be a cinch to catch the killer because we'll see it happen."

"What makes you think someone else is going to die?" Jack asked.

Rob held up his hands defensively. "What? I didn't say that, did I? I was just trying to lighten the mood. Dinner? Yes?"

Seeing as no one else had any better ideas, they followed Rob back down to the dining hall. It was fortunate that none of the food had been dished up, and that it was served on large, communal platters. However, there were a tense few moments after Rob took his first bite, where everyone pretended to be engrossed in pouring their drinks, or examining the Christmas crackers.

"Still alive! I told you it would be fine," Rob said, a second before all the lights went out.

They were plunged into darkness.

Holly shivered in the icy breeze, which had been enough to extinguish all of the candles a moment before. She nearly jumped out of her skin when a loud bang echoed around the room.

There was a moment of dead silence.

"I don't suppose that was someone pulling a cracker?" Rob enquired.

Someone near Holly swore - probably when they realised Rob wasn't the victim.

"I think it was a gunshot," Jack said.

There was another bang, not as loud or as fatal as the first. Holly suspected Rob had just hit his head on the table.

A SHOT IN THE DARK

Holly heard Rob mutter 'Hey presto' under his breath when the lights flickered and came back on. The person seated next to her remained silent.

That was because they were dead.

"Oh no, Lawrence…" Emma said, her voice emotionless. But then, during the very brief time Holly had known Lawrence, he had never inspired any particular emotion at all.

So, why would anyone want to kill him?

"I feel sick…" Lydia said. She pushed her chair back, sitting with her head between her legs and taking deep breaths.

Holly looked back at Lawrence and found that Lydia's reaction was not unreasonable. She was glad that she hadn't got around to eating her dinner yet.

She also wasn't going to be eating it anytime soon.

Her food hadn't escaped the event unscathed. She looked down in horror at all of the… bits.

Jack walked round the table to have a look. "Shot from behind…" he immediately said and then looked up and down the side of the table where Lawrence had sat. His eyes fell on Emma, who sat on one side of the dead man, and then they stayed fixed on Holly herself. "Have you got anything on you to prove that you aren't a psychopath who has come here to kill us all?" His voice was deadpan.

Holly didn't know if he was serious or not. "Uh... I..." She stumbled, wondering what she could possibly say or produce. An anti-psychopath ID card? These detectives had known each other for years. Wasn't it far more likely that it was one of them who was the killer? But then - albeit rarely - psychopaths did exist, so she understood the reason behind Jack's accusation.

She shook her head free from confusion. She knew she wasn't the killer!

"No way. I saw how pale she turned when she saw Pete. That was definitely her first dead body. She's not our killer," Emma cut in. Holly didn't know whether to thank her or throttle her.

"So... it's one of us. It must be someone on this side of the table. They had to get around behind old Lawrence and do him in," Jack said, his voice grave.

Emma glared at him. "*Do him in?* What is this... an Agatha Christie novel? You were on this side of the table, too. You're also a suspect and - much as I hate to admit it - you are the firearms expert. However... where you, or any one of us, have hidden the gun, I don't know," she finished.

Holly revised her opinion that Pete and Emma's rivalry was a big motive for murder. It would appear that Emma doled out her disdain in equal measures for all.

"Now... this might be a shot in the dark, but are we a hundred-percent sure that we're the only people here?" Rob ventured.

Everyone stared at him.

"What? It's a perfectly reasonable theory!" He frowned

and it slowly dawned on him. "Oh, right. It probably was too soon for that turn of phrase. Look, I'm sure Lawrence would want us to keep things upbeat. You know... if he wasn't dead."

"Maybe you're right," Lydia said, her voice sounding terrible and her face looking worse. Lawrence's death was clearly not sitting well with her. She raised her gaze to meet Rob's. "But, you know what? I'm not going to sit around here doing nothing. Your last theory that no one would die if we all sat together and ate dinner hasn't worked out. I'm going to conduct my own investigations. Alone. The way I always do." She winced. "Right after I've been sick." She stood up and hastened (surprisingly speed-ily, given the tightness of her dress) back towards the main stairway.

So much for safety in numbers, Holly thought.

"I don't really feel festive anymore," Jack grumbled, pushing himself away from the table and walking after Lydia.

"I'd better go and make sure he hasn't gone to kill her," Emma said. Her tone was sarcastic, but her expression wasn't. Trust wasn't particularly high amongst the profes-sional private detectives.

Holly, Miranda, and Rob were left sitting alone in the dining room with the very dead Lawrence for company.

"What are we going to do with the body?" Rob asked, in the same tone of voice you might use to propose a post-dinner game of charades. Miranda blinked a few times but said nothing (her horror akin to an unsuspecting person being invited to play charades).

"We could put the bodies outside to stave off decomposi-tion?" Holly suggested, wondering why she seemed to be thinking so clearly now. She was still seated next to some pretty gruesome remains, and her white dress had turned out to be a truly disastrous colour to choose, but all in all, she seemed pretty okay. She was alive. That definitely counted for something.

"Ah. I just meant I've got a Santa hat that we could use. I'd suggest a paper crown, but it probably won't cover much," Rob said, looking serious and thoughtful. Holly was starting to wonder if he was actually insane and somehow no one had noticed.

As if reading her mind, Rob spoke again. "By the way, I'm the sane one. It's the others you want to worry about. Also yes, yes I am very attractive," he said, with his fingers on his temples, staring at Holly with a smirk on his face.

She rolled her eyes, beginning to realise why the others in the group exercised their eyeballs so often. Of course, if they were very unlucky, they'd all be bouncing out of their heads and rolling across the floor soon. She gulped. Perhaps she wasn't thinking straight after all. "Er, we should probably…"

"Get dessert?" Rob finished. "Great idea!"

Holly looked from Lawrence to Miranda and realised they had to get the traumatised organiser out of the room. Or rather, she had to. Rob was already in the kitchen hunting for the next course.

"It hasn't been cooked yet," Miranda said, her voice a whisper when Holly half-walked, half-carried her out of the dining room, back towards the living room.

"The dessert… it was going to be warm chocolate fudge… cake." Between the words 'fudge' and 'cake' Miranda burst into tears. Holly was left with a dress that was not only plain and splattered with debris, but was now also wet and in danger of turning see-through.

"Found some cheese… no dessert, just powder. Even I'm not desperate enough to snort chocolate cake mix. See you girls later. Don't do anything I wouldn't do!" He hesitated in the doorway with an entire block of cheddar in his hand. "There's actually not a lot I wouldn't do. Try not to kill anyone or, you know... die. I guess we'll count up in the morning and then we'll try my suggestion. We'll search this house from bottom to top, because I'm smart, and I'm nearly always..." He paused, lost in thought. "No... wait. I'm always right. Yeah, that's it," Rob finished.

"Count up?" Miranda said, her face somehow turning a shade paler.

Holly forced a laugh, which came out alarmingly high-pitched. "He's kidding, aren't you, Rob? No one else is going to die." She shot him a meaningful look, but he wasn't even looking her way.

"Well, we are all going to die one day. Just... maybe some sooner than others," he concluded. Unsurprisingly, his reassuring speech did nothing to stop a fresh flood of tears from spilling down Holly's dress.

"I think you should go to bed now," she suggested, wondering if she could get away with outright telling him to get lost.

Rob cheerily waved the cheese at her. "All right. I'm going. Just a heads-up, don't come into my room tonight. There'll be numerous deadly booby traps set up, and don't take it personally, but I'm not telling you what they are. Heck, I probably won't even tell myself... just to make things more interesting." He wandered off down the corridor.

Holly turned to see that Miranda had calmed down a little. "On the plus side, there's a good chance he won't be down for breakfast," she told the organiser.

"I heard that!" Rob shouted from the corridor, before finally walking up the stairs.

"I must say, being snowed in with a bunch of people who keep getting murdered is not exactly what I expected my prize to be," Holly said to break the silence when she and Miranda were finally alone.

"Oh, I'm so sorry this has happened. I would never have

planned it here if I'd thought… " Miranda sighed, completely missing Holly's weak attempt at humour. "This is just terrible!"

"It's fine. Really," Holly said, trying to make the other woman feel better. Nothing about this situation was fine. "At least we still have… electricity. Most of the time," she added, reaching around for a silver-lining, before remembering what had happened earlier when Lawrence had been shot. "Come on, we're probably not in danger anyway, right? We aren't detectives!" In truth, Holly had no idea as to the motive behind the crimes, or if there was any pattern. One of their number could just be wiping the rest out for fun.

Holly's mind danced back to Emma's feud with Pete, and then Jack's logic that only someone sitting on the same side of the table as Lawrence could have killed him - and then had time to return to their seat without anyone noticing before the lights came on again. Jack had also been sat on that side of the table, meaning that he was a suspect too. Miranda had been standing when it had happened, so she was also under scrutiny. Although… Holly couldn't really bring herself to think of the tear-stained organiser as a brutal killer. *Appearances can be deceiving*, she reminded herself and wondered if she was sat alone in the room with the killer.

Where is the gun? the voice inside her head queried. She still couldn't figure out how anyone could have managed to conceal a gun after killing Lawrence in time for the lights to come back on.

"I… I suppose you're right. These seven detectives, sorry - six - have met for a few years. Maybe one of them has gone crazy. They are under such a lot of pressure," Miranda said - as if being under pressure excused violent murder.

"I'm sure no one could ever want you dead," Holly said to comfort the other woman, but was a bit miffed when the organiser didn't return the sentiment.

"You're right. I've nothing to do with any of this! At least we're in the company of great detectives. One of them will figure it out," Miranda said, brightening up.

"Yeah, you bet!" Holly said, privately thinking that if there was anyone she'd consider well-qualified to plan and commit the perfect crime, it would be a private detective. The way the deaths had happened... they weren't impulsive. This had all been carefully plotted.

And Holly was starting to wonder where she personally fitted into the deadly drama.

SCOOBY DOO

Holly did not sleep very well. A double murder has a way of making it hard to drop off into dreamland.

For the first few hours, she'd lain in her bed staring up at the ceiling, listening to the sounds of the old house creaking. Once or twice, it had creaked so much she'd wondered if there was a ghost somewhere up in the rafters. That thought hadn't made her sleep any easier - especially given the possibility that there were two brand-new ghosts running around the old house.

When she finally opened her eyes (after what felt like five minutes of sleep) and looked out of the window, the world was still white. It was only now the storm had been vanquished that she realised how much snow had fallen. Judging by a telegraph pole she could see in the distance, the entire bottom floor of Horn Hill House must now be under several feet of snow. She tried not to think about the state her car would be in. Her insurance might not cover galavanting off to Scotland in ridiculous weather conditions.

She was just thinking how muffled everything sounded

when there was snow on the ground, when a scream cut through the air. The little voice inside her head whispered '*And so it begins*' but Holly was already running out of her room and onto the landing.

Emma White stood in the corridor, her hand still resting on the handle of the door she'd just pulled open.

Before Holly could reach her side, she turned and spoke. "I was just going to ask if she wanted breakfast. Miranda is downstairs making it. I offered to wake people up. I'd almost forgotten…" Emma finished, her voice getting quieter at the end until no sound came out.

Holly nodded understandingly. She inched towards the room, being careful to steer clear of Emma. Perhaps it was paranoia, but when you were staying in a house with seven other people, and they kept dying, one by one, exercising a little caution was a healthy attitude to hold onto.

"What happened to her?" Holly asked, frowning at the inert form on the floor of the bedroom. Lydia Burns didn't look nearly as polished as she usually did. Her hair was dishevelled and wavy, and her face - which was devoid of makeup and her trademark red lips - looked a strange shade of green. Holly stepped forwards for a closer look… and then retreated just as quickly when the smell hit her. It initially smelt like expensive perfume, with hints of spice and leather, but there was something off about it. Why was it present in such pungent quantities? Had Lydia spilt a container when she'd died?

"The perfume…" Emma said and started backing away in horror. She dragged a bewildered Holly after her, so they were both out of the room. "Poisoned perfume. Breathing it in directly must be enough to kill you! Whoever is doing this… they must have persuaded Lydia to use it, or smell it, or something. Remember when she said she felt ill last night? It could already have been happening then."

Holly tried not to let her knees shake too much. She'd just taken a big whiff of the very thing that may have been responsible for Lydia Burns' death, and she hadn't had a clue! "Thanks, I might have stayed in there too long, or even touched it, if it weren't for you," Holly said, wondering why something was jumping up and down in the back of her mind. She couldn't seem to catch hold of the unreachable thought.

"What the heck is all of the noise?" Jack Dewfall strode out his room, already dressed in a tailored military-esque suit. Holly wondered if he wore it to bed.

"Lydia's dead," Emma said without a trace of the emotion she'd displayed to Holly.

Jack just nodded in acceptance. "I assumed that would probably be the case. One of us was bound to die in the night. The killer is keeping this to a tight schedule."

Holly felt like smacking him around the head. If he'd had a theory, why hadn't he shared it sooner?

"Case... cases... this is to do with cases!" Holly said, thinking out loud, as her brain finally connected the dots. "Pete's most successful case of the past year was that knife-crime gang he stopped." Emma made a noise of derision and muttered something about them being harmless schoolgirls, but Holly ploughed on. "Lawrence's case was probably an assassination attempt of some type, right? And Lydia... Lydia solved the lipstick murders, where models were being poisoned by their lipstick. Now she's been poisoned by perfume. She may not have even worn it. Perhaps it was in her room already in a bottle designed to leak, or someone might have crept in last night and covered her mouth and nose with it while she slept, just to finish the job." Holly bit her lip, unsure if she wanted to analyse exactly how Lydia had met her end. It seemed all too likely that similar ends were planned for the rest of the detectives.

"Yeah, I was thinking that, too," Emma said, nodding like it was obvious.

Jack mimicked the movement. "Pretty clear when you think about it."

Holly felt crushed for a second, before she realised what they were doing. Despite a murderer picking them off, these detectives were still in competition and could never concede anything to anyone in their field of work. Holly tried not to sigh too loudly. It was probably partially due to their own arrogance that they'd been caught out. But the real question still remained: Who was murdering the detectives, and why?

She was about to open her mouth to put that question to them when Rob strolled around the corner, dressed in a fluffy rabbit-print onesie. On anyone else, it would have looked ridicu... Wait.

No.

It still looked ridiculous. Even with Rob Frost wearing it.

"Did someone say breakfast?" Rob asked, smiling benignly around.

"No one said breakfast," Jack corrected, his mouth set in a grim line of disapproval.

Rob frowned and scratched his head. "No, someone definitely said it approximately five minutes ago. It was before you all started talking about horrible Lydia's death?" He frowned. "Or is that Lydia's horrible death? It's too early for good syntax."

Rob looked around at the blank faces and fixed his gaze on Holly. "Nice work on the case theory. It seems to fit. It's so obvious that we all completely missed it!" He laughed in what seemed a genuine manner and headed for the stairs.

Holly frowned at the backhanded compliment. You couldn't win with these people!

"Come on, if we wait any longer, one of us will have died before we can dish up the scrambled eggs!" he called back.

The detectives standing on the landing shrugged and followed him.

Miranda's worried expression was immediately replaced by her usual sunny smile when they poked their heads into the kitchen.

"Good morning, I've already set the table in the, ah… main room," she faltered, her mind clearly flashing back to the violent demise of Lawrence Richards and his final resting place in the dining room - where he presumably still sat, face down in his stone-cold dinner. A different group of people would probably have moved him, or covered him as a mark of respect, but Holly suspected that these detectives had concluded that they wanted everything as untouched as possible. They must already be deep into their own investigations. It was just too bad that none of them trusted her enough to share their ideas, and with the way they were dropping like flies, it didn't look likely that their trust would be increasing anytime soon.

"Thanks Miranda," Holly deliberately said, after they'd filed into the room and crowded around the large, but rather low, coffee table. The blonde organiser looked startled for a second, and then shrugged, like whipping up a full English breakfast had been a piece of cake. *Perhaps it was,* Holly thought, remembering last night's packaging and wondering if there was such a thing as a re-heatable breakfast. She decided she'd rather not know.

"Great job everyone! We've made it through a meal with no one dying," Rob said when they'd all finished eating and were drinking the filter coffees that Miranda had again brought out all by herself. Holly wondered how much she was getting paid.

"Shut up, Rob," Jack said, without batting an eyelid. "We need to get to the bottom of this right here and right now. Yesterday, we were all tired and we ran out of time. Today is a new day, and it's not the day that I am dying." The heavy detective leaned forwards and spread his hands wide on the table. "I'm proposing a mission for help. The white stuff is pretty deep out there, but the blizzard has ended. I'll go for help while you all wait here. Then we'll get to the bottom of this matter." He eyeballed them each in turn, his thoughts visible on his face. *Whichever one of you is the murderer, you aren't getting me.*

He stood up and went to grab his coat, returning a few seconds later looking even more like the *Michelin Man* in his down jacket.

"You all hang tight and try not to kill each other. I'll be back before you know it," he said, leaving the other detectives, Miranda, and Holly no time to argue. He thrust open the large French doors, letting the snowdrift fall in, where it formed a big pile at his feet. Miranda squeaked in protest (presumably because of the venue deposit) but then stuffed a fist in her mouth. Jack turned around to grin at them all, one final time, the military genius about to go on another rescue mission.

"See you later, suckers!" he said and trudged up the hill of white powder. They could all just see his feet through the top of the glass doors, walking away across the snow into the distance.

The glass doors rattled when an explosion sent the snow, and whatever remained of Jack, high up into the air. When the white powder cleared, all they could see were Jack's boots, one still upright on the snow. The rest of Jack was gone.

"I did not see *that* coming," Rob said, his mouth the mirror image of the three other gaping holes in the room. Rob tilted his head. "With hindsight, it seems rather obvious, doesn't it? He's a military detective. Boom. Landmine." Rob glanced, nervously, at the boots in the snow. "Having said that, I'm not going to assume that there was just the one landmine that Jack happened to step on. I reckon we're stuck here until whatever happens, happens."

"So, we're all going to die," Emma said.

Miranda choked on her coffee. "There are only four of us left. One of us has got to be the murderer. Isn't that right?" she said, surprising everyone by having an opinion.

Holly resisted the urge to yell 'not it!', knowing that everyone would claim the same - whether guilty or innocent. "We still aren't certain that we're on our own here," Holly reminded them, remembering the creaking noises she'd heard last night. "Is there an attic? We should start there. If not an attic, the cellar…"

Emma and Miranda made sounds of agreement, but Rob just rolled his eyes. "Why does it always take someone else to make the same suggestion I've made for people to actually do it?" He shook his head.

Holly felt guilty for a second, before Rob flashed her a genuine smile. "Don't worry about it," he said, dropping out of character for once. "So gang, let's split up and solve this mystery! Daphne and I will take the attic. Shaggy and Scooby, you're down in the cellar. If there is such a thing…" he said, reaching out and pulling Holly to his side. Apparently, she was Daphne, although she'd always considered herself more of a Velma. She was the smart one of the group.

"Shut up, Fred," Emma said, before stalking out of the room with a baffled looking Miranda trailing behind her.

"Excellent! I'm sure absolutely nothing at all will go wrong with this plan," Rob said, his tone dry.

JUST LIKE NANCY DREW

"Any idea where the attic could be in a big old pile like this one?" Rob asked as they hiked up the stairs.

"Somewhere near the top of the house?" Holly offered, her mind still going through the deaths of the four other detectives. She was trying to piece together something - anything - that would give them a clue as to what was going on.

"No kidding, Sherlock," Rob commented, but Holly was starting to notice that even his usual humour seemed strained. It was as if he could sense his own death approaching.

Now that she thought about it, Holly wasn't feeling so great herself. So far, it had only been the detectives who'd been targeted, but without knowing the motive behind these murders, it could still be open season on them all. Perhaps the killer was just an exceedingly creative psychopath.

"Hey, I hope you didn't mind being assigned to attic duty. I just don't want to go anywhere that could be classed as underground right now," Rob said.

Holly nodded. At least one of them had figured a few things out. "None of this makes sense," she commented rhetorically.

"Welcome to my world. It always feels that way until you crack the thing open. Usually, you've got a bit more breathing space. This case is more along the lines of how many breaths do we have left? Ah-ha!" Rob said, when the broom handle they were using to check the ceilings finally knocked on something hollow.

"If that's a loft hatch, it looks like someone papered over it years ago," Holly observed, squinting up at the apparently flawless ceiling.

Rob rubbed his stubbly chin. "Or that's what someone *wants* us to think," he said, grabbing a sturdy looking - probably very valuable - antique table and placing it beneath the suspected entrance. "Hi-yah!" he yelled, jamming the broom handle up and tearing a hole through the thick paper. He ripped the rest apart. Then, with an admirable lack of hesitation, he pushed open the loft hatch. Rob placed it back down a couple of seconds later.

Holly discovered she'd been holding her breath.

"Yeah, uh... it probably was covered up for years. There is absolutely nothing up there. All I could see was a broken window, and it looks like birds or bats might use it as a roost," he said. Holly wondered if that was what she'd heard last night. It sounded likely.

Rob looked up at the rip in the ceiling. "Hmm, if we use a bit of sticky tape, they might not notice?"

Holly bit her lip but said nothing. If they all died at Horn Hill House, a ruined ceiling would hardly be anything to worry about.

"Look, I've been thinking some more," Holly said when they walked back down the stairs, hoping to find two not-dead people waiting for them in the living room.

"Thinking is a good thing to get into the habit of doing," Rob said, probably for the sake of hearing his voice out loud.

"Whoever has been killing detectives obviously knows you well and knows all of your cases, right? How many people can know all of that stuff?" she asked, and then realised how silly it sounded. She herself had found out tons just by searching for the detectives on the internet.

She blushed and carried on before Rob could tell her she was nutty. "I mean, I know there's general information out there, but how could they know that Jack would be the one to go for a rescue mission? Or that Pete was going to take a nap? Or even that Lawrence would be sitting at the table and not decide to move, or something like that?" She wondered if it could possibly be that - so far - the murderer had just had an unfair share of dumb luck.

The more she thought about it, the more it didn't feel right. It was as if everything had been planned and put in place before they'd even come to Horn Hill...

"Hey, Rob... How much do you trust Tom March?" she asked, remembering the seventh detective who had cancelled at the last minute.

Rob's expression immediately darkened. Holly wondered if she might have just hit the nail on the head. "Well, it's probably him, Miranda, or Emma... I took the liberty of excluding myself, because I know I didn't do it, and you, because I actually suggested the competition that you won. Hmm... I suppose you could be a genius at computers and have fixed it so you could win somehow, just so you could come up here and kill us all." He frowned. "Probably not, right? We were just alone together for ages and you didn't try anything. There was no hint of an evil mastermind speech at all. Unless I talked over it. Did I talk over it? I have a habit of doing that."

Holly shook her head, just to reassure him. "Why did you suggest the competition?" she asked, genuinely curious. She'd assumed it was Miranda's idea - probably in an effort to gain some sane company for herself over the weekend.

Rob shrugged. "I thought it would be nice to have someone come in from the outside world who might not pick holes in our stories the way other detectives do. That and I also thought that just in case someone decides to kill us all off, wouldn't it be great to add in an extra target to buy myself a little more time? I'm very forward thinking like that."

"Thanks a bunch," Holly muttered.

"What were you doing up there? You took forever!" Miranda greeted them when they walked back into the living room. The organiser suddenly dissolved into blushes. Rob grinned, enjoying every second of her and Holly's discomfort.

"Nothing but bats and birds and, ah... a slightly ripped ceiling to report," Rob said, deliberately avoiding eye contact with Miranda.

"We found nothing, too," Emma said, and then quickly added: "Miranda and I made cake," before the organiser could ask the questions she so clearly wanted to about the ceiling.

Emma held out a plate towards Rob, who took it eagerly.

"I needed something chocolate so badly. I'm afraid I couldn't resist," Miranda said, raising a plate containing her half-eaten piece of sticky cake.

The next moment, she was dead.

Rob dropped his fork a second after Miranda dropped to the floor.

"Of all things sacred and holy..." he muttered and stared longingly at his plate of cake. "Fudge!" he cursed... or perhaps he was just identifying the type of cake. It wasn't very clear. Emma said a different word beginning with 'f' that was definitely not 'fudge'.

"Why would anyone want to poison Miranda?" Holly asked, hoping her curiosity wasn't callous.

Emma and Rob exchanged a glance.

"Well…" Emma grudgingly began, after Rob had shaken his head and mimed placing crosses in front of himself a few times to indicate he didn't want to speak. "Miranda wasn't exactly a detective, but she was a super-fan. You might have missed it…" Holly wasn't sure if that was sarcasm or not. "Anyway, we've allowed Miranda to put these little meetings together for us for a couple of years now. She loves hearing about our cases and we…" She cleared her throat. "…well, these meetings can be interesting for us, too."

Rob unhelpfully mimed being overcome with gratitude at the almost - but not really - complement.

"There was one case that Miranda cracked all on her own," Rob cut in, but Emma shot him a glare that clearly said he'd given up his right to tell this story.

"Being a super-fan, she was the only one who figured out that the mastermind behind seven different murders was actually the same person. It just so happened that we were each working on the individual murders in our own different ways. It was that case which brought us all together. Miranda solved it, and after she solved it, she made us a chocolate cake to celebrate. From then on, well… she's always made the cake," Emma said, starting to sound a little bit choked-up.

"So… it *is* someone who knows you really well," Holly deduced, feeling simultaneously alarmed and relieved.

There was no way a stranger would have known about Miranda's connection with cake. Someone with a personal grudge against the detectives was definitely targeting them, and she personally had no history with them. There was surely no reason for her to die. That didn't change the fact that two detectives were still alive, one of the seven was missing from the meeting all together, and it was pretty obvious that something was going to happen to reduce their number even further.

The silence stretched out as the others thought through the same facts.

"It's probably Tom," Emma said, voicing all of their growing suspicions aloud. "But why? And also… how? We've searched the house."

Holly had just opened her mouth to say something when they all heard a crash from upstairs. Emma's reaction was to sprint from the room in the direction of the sound. She was already gone by the time Holly shouted at her to stop.

There was a burst of machine gun fire and the sound of running footsteps was cut short.

"Tommy Gun mystery," Holly and Rob said together, exchanging a horrified look. They didn't want to go and see what had happened to Emma, but just in case… in case she'd somehow made it… they had to. They had to see what had happened and see if it got them any closer to solving this case, before it reached its very final conclusion.

"Where did the machine gun fire even come from?" Rob mused when they stepped out into the hall, both treading carefully to avoid the spreading pool of blood that surrounded the late Emma White - another detective mown down by the twisted fiend behind these murders.

Holly quickly glanced at the bullet holes and then back up in the direction she supposed they must have come from. All she could see was a wooden panel, much like any of the hundreds of other similar panels that decorated the interior.

"What if everything that has happened was set up in advance? What if someone's been watching us all along without actually being here at all?" she said, feeling the cold dread of realisation washing over her.

"Tom... Tom was always good with technology," Rob growled, his hands twitching nervously.

"I have an idea. Let's go back to my room while we figure out what to do next," Holly suggested. "I probably won't have been targeted, will I? Also, there aren't any tunnels or anything like bank vaults in my room... and how would anyone have predicted that you'd end up in there?" she finished.

Rob raised an eyebrow.

Holly just crossed her arms and gave him a death stare. Now was really not the time!

"You could have picked any room," she said and immediately blushed when she heard her own words. "I didn't mean..." She sighed and trailed after Rob, whose chest seemed to have puffed up to double its usual size.

They both sat on Holly's four-poster bed, staring out at the snow in the distance. The snow closer to the house featured a huge crater and rather a lot of staining. They didn't look at it.

"So... things are triggered, and we're probably being watched. Listened to as well, I guess," Holly said, glancing at Rob for approval. To her, this sounded way too much like being in a bad spy movie.

"Yeah... who knows, right? I don't do technology. I just get in the bad guys' heads and then get my spade out and dig," he said, miming digging. "Now Emma... she was great with tech! Always knew how to program my iPod. Jack, too. He was very into it with all the military stuff. And Lawrence... the sort of gear he had to track targets and isolate threats - well, it boggles my mind!" He sort of trailed off. "Come to think of it, everyone here - even Miranda - was brilliant at technology - apart from me. They'd probably have been able to figure all of this out a lot sooner, if they'd lived. That's probably why I'm still alive," he added brightly, and then frowned, remembering that while ignorance had kept him alive so far, there was still the big finale to come. "How are you with technology? Could you hack their system and turn it back on them, or something like that? I don't know what I'm saying. It just sounds good."

Holly gritted her teeth. "Nope. If you want a piano played, I'm the one to call. I can send email and do the usual everyday stuff on a computer, but not much more. I definitely don't know about any of this hi-tech surveillance stuff." She looked round at Rob, but he didn't even appear to be listening.

He was crouched in front of the bookshelf. "We should start checking for bugs. Having said that, I have no idea what one looks like, so we probably won't know if we find one. Whoops!" His hand had brushed the spine of one of the rather weathered books and it fell face-down onto the rug. There was a dull metallic thunk when it landed.

Rob and Holly looked at each other for a long, silent second.

"Nancy Drew," Rob said, reading the spine. "It looks like your name was on the kill list after all." He gingerly lifted the book. Holly looked down at the sharp metal barb, which was so firmly embedded in the floor, the rug was now pinned to the floorboards. If she'd opened the book, it would have fired straight into her face.

"They're all amateur detective novels," Rob noted, inspecting the spines of the remaining books.

Holly gulped, probably audibly. If they hadn't been running around the house, she'd almost certainly have picked one up to read. That sort of book was her favourite. Someone had either known it, or was a very good guesser.

"Why would anyone want me dead?" she mused, thinking wildly back to the dog-fighting ring and the mayor's stolen chain. Neither of those cases seemed worthy of a death vendetta.

Rob shrugged. "Maybe our killer wanted a clean sweep. By the way, it would be awesome if you could let me know if you see anything that looks threatening or deadly and at all related to my cases. Just a heads-up," he said casually, but Holly wasn't fooled by his cool act. She may have narrowly avoided death thanks to Rob's clumsiness, but his own ending was still imminent.

"We may have semi-solved the mystery. Your old friend Tom isn't really your friend. But we're still probably going to die," Holly concluded, chewing that one over.

The traps that had killed all of the other detectives may still be loaded. They'd need to watch themselves around the machine gun area and the room where Lawrence had been assassinated. And who knew? There could be more death traps hanging around the place - just in case any of the original attempts had failed.

"What do we do now?" Holly pulled out her phone and stared again at the tiny 'no service' message on the screen.

"I can think of a few things…" Rob said.

Holly shot him a warning look.

"Do you think that cake was a hundred-percent poisoned, or just the sponge itself? Maybe if I only ate the icing…" the last detective standing mused.

"Maybe there is no death trap for you because the person doing this to us knew that, if you were left alone for long enough, you'd eventually find a way to kill yourself with no help needed."

Rob frowned. "Now is not the time to flirt with me!"

Holly was about to protest, but he was already on his feet, looking out of the window. Not so subtly, his hand searched around the window pane edges until...

"Ah-ha!" he said, pulling off what looked like a blob of congealed dirt to Holly, but turned out to have little wires attached to it. "This is definitely a... something. What are the chances that it's the only one?" They searched some more, but found nothing further, except for the strong possibility that Holly's bathroom mirror contained a concealed camera - something which completely grossed her out.

"I guess that we should hope for the best and talk plans," Rob said in a low voice that they both prayed wouldn't carry. "I say we make a run for it."

Holly's eyes were immediately drawn down to the snow that surrounded the house. "Following in Jack's footsteps," she muttered.

Rob winced. "I know it's chancy, but we can't stay here forever, or that chocolate cake is going to start looking real good. I mean, it already does. But, you know - even better."

"No, I mean really follow in his footsteps. Until he hit the landmine, he was fine. Hopefully we will be, too," Holly explained.

Rob's face brightened a little. "Hey, that is a point! Too bad Jack only made it a few steps before 'boom'. But it is a start."

Holly chewed her lip, wondering if this really was the only way. But with decomposing bodies for company and no more poison-free food, they didn't have much choice. Unfortunately, she suspected that the perpetrator of this massacre would have realised as much.

"It seems as good a time as any to die," Rob said, pushing himself up off the bed and walking out the door.

Holly made to move after him and then sat down again.

He shot her a sympathetic look. "Take your time, I'll wait," he assured her.

She nodded absently, her eyes still fixed on the distant, perfect, undisturbed snow. She walked back over to the window and ran her hand across the spines of the books, lost in thought.

Rob looked up when she finally exited the room.

"I just had another thought," she told him.

LUCKY NUMBER SEVEN

Old houses tended to have their fair share of junk. Holly knew it was time to brave the cellar and go in search of it.

Rob waited nervously in the living room, trying to pretend that Miranda wasn't face-down on the floor. They'd both agreed it would be a pretty stupid idea for him to go into the cellar. Holly wasn't convinced it was one of her most brilliant plans either, but Miranda and Emma had visited and returned unscathed. She could only hope that the same would be true for her... and that she'd be able to find something that fit the idea she had in her head.

A few tennis rackets and strips of twine later, they had what they needed - makeshift snowshoes.

"Nice work, Miss *Blue Peter*, but how does this help? Beyond giving the forensics a good laugh..." Rob asked, looking dubiously at his feet. They were standing in front of the sodden carpet, where the snowdrift Jack had let in had since melted.

"Jack went out in his combat boots, right? The mines were either buried during the storm, or maybe even before it.

After all - the bad guy couldn't bank on there being snow to keep us all here. It's probable that they were laid right after we all arrived. So maybe they had to do it in the snow? I guess there's also a chance it was done before all the snow and then - I don't know - activated later? Is that a thing with landmines?" she asked and shuddered, half from cold, half from the thought that she may have already walked over a landmine that contained enough explosive to vaporise her. And she hadn't known a thing about it.

"My bet would be that they did all of this long before we arrived. This killer doesn't leave a lot to chance," Rob concluded, still frowning at his tennis rackets.

"The theory of the shoes is that they'll spread our weight. There's a chance we may be light enough to not trigger the mines. It probably won't work, but I just thought... every little helps," Holly said, thinking more and more that this had been a stupid idea. Actually, the whole wanting to be a real detective and driving up to Scotland for this convention had been a stupid idea, but there was no time to dwell on that.

She had an appointment with death.

They crawled up the steep incline of snow, both holding their breath after every movement. Eventually, they were standing on top of the white stuff, looking at the crater where Jack had met his end.

"Ladies first?" Rob heroically suggested. Holly glared at him. They both stared at the red stain on the snow for a bit longer, before they furiously played rock, paper, scissors.

Holly won.

"Best of three?" Rob asked, but Holly crossed her arms.

The first few metres went fine. Holly's theory about following in Jack's footsteps held out, and it was only when they reached the spot where Jack had died that things went a bit pear-shaped.

"I suppose we should go round," Holly suggested, trying

not to be sick from the smell of blood and... other things... which were starting to defrost, along with the snow.

"Into the unknown we go," Rob muttered and shuffled around the edge of the hole, casting nervous glances in its direction. Holly followed him.

They made it another two metres before it finally happened.

"Boom!" a voice shouted. They both nearly jumped out of their skin. A burst of maniacal laughter travelled across the snow and they looked back in the direction of the house, to see a man striding around the side towards them.

Where he'd come from, Holly didn't know, but she had a feeling that they really didn't want to stick around to find out.

"Run!" she hissed at Rob, but it turned out to be quite a challenge to do anything more than a steady waddle in their tennis racket shoes. Holly wondered if she'd slowed them down for nothing. The man was walking easily across the snow, like there was nothing to worry about. *Perhaps he just knows where all of the mines are*, she thought. She wondered if they could take him out and then follow his footsteps back to safety. Unfortunately, if he was willing to show himself to them, it probably meant that there was zero chance of their survival.

Just to prove her right, Rob made a strangled screaming sound and promptly fell to his death.

Or he would have done, if Holly hadn't been semi-expecting it and grabbed the back of his coat, swinging him a little to the left with a gargantuan effort.

"Unnngh!" said Rob, which might have translated into: 'Thanks for mostly saving me'. Alternatively, it might have meant: 'There are spiky things in this pit that just opened up, and I'm still hanging over it'. The latter was unfortunately true. While Holly had done enough to keep Rob from outright falling into the previously concealed pit, he was now braced over the abyss… and the snow around the edges looked like it could give way at any second. Holly hoped that he was as in-shape as he looked, because his core strength was about to be tested.

"Tom March, I presume?" Holly said, turning to face the newcomer, hoping that if she blocked his vision of Rob, Rob could quietly work on getting himself out of the sticky situation.

A gun glinted in the bright afternoon sunshine, looking dark and deadly. The man standing in front of her slowly clapped against the back of the hand that held the gun, the cruel smile not leaving his face. Holly looked at the person she'd assumed to be the face of evil and found he actually looked quite normal. His hair was pale and ashy and his face was quite pleasant, if it hadn't been for that smile. Holly looked into his blue eyes and didn't see what she'd expected, but that just went to show…

"Come on, Rob, be a sport and let go. If you end it now, I'll let your girlfriend live," Tom called.

"No need to keep her alive, she's nothing to me,'" Rob said, perhaps mishearing Tom, or perhaps choosing completely the wrong moment to display his usual dark sense of humour. Holly only just resisted kicking him in the ribs.

It would have been a very fatal kick.

"Nice to meet you, Tom. Killing the other detectives so you could be the brightest and best, huh? That's pretty clever!" she said, trying to play for time.

Fortunately, Tom was more than happy to gloat. "I hated these stupid meetings. Every time, it was always: 'Boast about your greatest case, while the others pick holes and point out how they would have done it all a hundred times better'. Who needs that?" He shook his head.

Behind her, Holly heard Rob sigh. "I know you had a bit of a dry year, Tom, but that's no reason to take it out on us. I thought we were buddies?" Rob said, still hanging precariously over the death pit.

"I hate you. I've told you that several times," Tom said.

"Yeah, sure you have! Like... in the friendly way," Rob replied.

Tom ignored him. "Anyway, this was all a great idea. It's Christmas come early for me! Now, if you'll just be helpful and die, that would be lovely. It was all planned so that you would die last, Rob. I always hated you the most with your easy money cases. I bet you creamed cash from every single one, too! Who's going to miss a few million when hundreds of millions of pounds worth of gold is recovered and returned?"

Rob laughed as delicately as possible. "Have you seen the clothes I wear? And if you saw my house, you wouldn't... Hey! You *can* see my house! Let's go there now and have a cup of tea. I guarantee you'll feel far less homicidal after a good brew."

Tom shook his head. "You are a terrible smooth talker. How have you lived this long?" He snorted. "Oh yes, I forgot. You're more of an amateur metal-detector enthusiast than a true detective."

Rob grumbled something about being better at his job than Tom was, but he didn't get to finish. Tom had balled up a snowball and managed to aim it past Holly. It smacked Rob's thigh and caused him to jerk dangerously over the deadly pit.

"What am I saying? You're amazing! You were always the best of us. You can be the leader of every detective meeting we have from now on. How about you let me up?" Rob wheedled.

"Smooth," Holly muttered under her breath, unable to see

any way out of this. She had one final trick up her sleeve, but she was willing to bet that Tom was a quicker draw than she was, and she would only have one chance…

"Where do we go from here?" Holly asked, hoping that the more Tom talked, the more he'd lose his focus.

To her dismay, he raised his gun. "I think I'll shoot you backwards into the pit. You'll make Rob fall to his death and you'll both be impaled. It seems the most efficient way to end this. It's nothing personal. You were never my competition, Holly, but you know who I am, etcetera, etcetera. It would be inconvenient if you lived to tell anyone that I was the one who engineered this series of untimely endings. It would certainly ruin things when I drive up here tomorrow only to discover that - oh no! All of my old friends are dead, leaving me the country's best private detective. I'll clean up," he added with a grin. "I'll clean up business-wise, I mean. Not the corpses." His nose wrinkled.

Holly realised that there was a reason he'd killed everyone remotely. Perhaps, deep down, he lacked the brutal resolve needed to murder with his own hands, or maybe he really despised seeing dead people. Either way, it gave her a chance…

Her hand twitched towards her pocket, but Tom was quicker. The gun came up and the sound of a final, fatal shot, echoed across the snowy landscape.

Holly opened one eye and cautiously looked down at her coat.

It was bright red.

But that was the colour it had been when she'd put it on to leave the house. There were no additional stains seeping through.

"Rob?" she called, her voice thin.

"Also not dead yet," came the reply, which left only one option. Holly looked in front of her at where Tom March lay face down. A pool of crimson was already spreading out through the snow.

"Did the idiot point it the wrong way or something?" Rob asked, sounding as baffled as Holly felt. She knelt and hauled upwards on his coat, giving him enough support to push himself up and away from the pit and its deadly spikes.

"No idea what happened, but how about we don't wait to find out?" Holly suggested and Rob nodded.

"Too bad he didn't happen to divulge any information about where the landmines are hidden during that annoying, evil monologue. Just our luck," Rob commented, brushing the snow off his knees.

Holly blinked as something silver reflected sunlight directly into her eyes.

"Don't move, or I'll shoot!" a familiar voice called across the snow.

Miranda emerged from the French doors and started walking towards them. The assault rifle she carried looked remarkably at home in her hands.

"Hey... wasn't she dead a minute ago?" Rob asked in a stage whisper.

Holly shrugged. She'd been pretty sure, but looking back, none of them had actually checked the woman's pulse. She'd just looked so... dead. The whole 'not moving' act had been very convincing. When you added one more death to the other murders, they'd all just made the assumption.

"I don't suppose you've just rescued us?" Rob asked hopefully.

Miranda laughed and shook her head. Something about the way her eyes glinted let Holly know she was no longer playing the part of sweet, fluffy Miranda - the super-fan who would do anything at all for her heroes. The woman in front of them was undoubtedly the real Miranda - the person she'd hidden from them all.

"No, this is actually the first wobble in the whole shebang. I thought Tom had already pulled the trigger when I shot him in the back. He probably hesitated, so he could talk some more. Blah blah blah, always going on." She looked down at the dead traitor detective with distaste. "He was a pretty poor villain. We don't really harp on about how life is unfair and how it's all everyone else's fault but our own that we're not achieving anything. Real criminals just get on with the job." She raised the gun to prove her point.

"Wait! Just one thing! You've got to tell us why you did it. Please? Last request?" Holly asked, hoping she didn't sound too pitiful.

Miranda rolled her eyes and glanced down at the highly expensive watch she was wearing. *Looking back, I suppose that watch was a bit out of place,* Holly thought, remembering Miranda's otherwise highly-planned eccentric and fluffy style of dress.

"All right. The condensed version only. I contacted all of the detectives and pretended to be Little Miss Super-Fan, who just wanted to help them solve a case. I did it so that I could keep tabs find out if any of them were close to uncovering my operations. I knew about the murder case I helped them to solve because of my underworld connections, and it was a pleasure to tip the detectives off about the killer. He was an operative of mine who'd become quite a thorn in my side. Obviously, I've had to accept a few losses, but knowing about the detectives' individual methods and the jobs they were on helped me to stay ahead - so they never caught the big game. Everything was great... until this year. Rob busted my biggest funding operation. He dug his way into one of my group's tunnels and ruined the whole heist. It was a job that had taken years of planning, and in a single afternoon, this idiot stumbled upon it. You weren't even looking for thieves, were you, Rob?" Miranda said, her voice cold.

Rob blushed a little. "Ah, well... not so much at the start, but after I found them, I was definitely looking for thieves."

Holly raised her eyebrows at him.

"I was hunting for something else, okay?" he told her.

She decided to leave it at that. If they lived through the next five minutes, they could chit-chat later.

"As I was saying... that was not in the plan. I realised that I had unknowingly been engineering the perfect scenario to end the era of private detectives. Now all I needed was a fall guy..." They all looked at Tom. Rob gave a little groan, probably regretting how easily Tom - and all of them - had been manipulated. Or, knowing Rob, perhaps he was just thinking about how that chocolate cake hadn't been poisoned after all.

"Oh no, this makes so much sense now," he said. Both women stared at him. "I should have figured it out sooner. You knew that Lawrence was going to be killed during the main course. That's why you hadn't bothered to bake the warm chocolate fudge cake. You already knew there wasn't going to be a dessert! I can't believe I didn't see it sooner."

Holly stuck her tongue into her cheek realising that (weirdly) Rob was right. Miranda shrugged as if it changed nothing... which it didn't.

"So, Tom turns out to be the murderer while you, Miranda the organiser, manage to escape the bloodbath and shoot Tom with a weapon you just happened to find lying around the house," Holly said, eyeing the assault rifle with skepticism. There was no way anyone was going to believe that one of those things had been easy to come by.

Next to her, Rob cleared his throat. "My rifle was in my bag," he muttered.

Holly felt her heart drop. She opened her mouth to ask why he'd brought it, but then didn't bother. For all she knew, the detectives brought their weapons with them, to show off how big and shiny they were. It wouldn't have surprised her. Why had she ever wanted to join their ranks?

"Rob, you are an idiot," Holly said, turning to stare at him - hopefully distracting Miranda from what her right hand was up to.

"Great last words," Miranda commented dryly, and hefted the gun.

Holly assumed she'd make it look like Tom had shot Rob and her, and then… Holly glanced at the gun in Tom's hand. She'd need to reach for that, if she really wanted this murder to look the part, otherwise it would be all wrong.

The gun she was holding in her hand wasn't the one she'd use for them.

She'd already shot Tom with it 'saving the day'.

She needed to pick the other gun up to kill them.

"Don't move," Miranda growled, probably reading her facial expressions. "I can see you're being Little Miss Smarty Pants, the amateur detective, but if this crime doesn't end up being perfect, so what? All I lose is my role of the tragic hero-ine. I'll just disappear and leave it as an unsolved massacre instead. I think we've chatted enough. Time to die," she said, levelling the gun.

AGATHA RAISIN

For a brief moment, Miranda had to look down to check the location of Tom's gun.

Holly knew it was her only chance.

She pulled the book free from her pocket and opened it up, keeping the spine towards her and the open pages pointed at Miranda. There was a twang when the spring loaded mechanism spat its deadly dart out. Aiming a book is a hard thing to do with any great degree of accuracy, but Holly had beginner's luck on her side.

The dart speared Miranda's temple and embedded itself deep in her brain. The mass murderer's hand squeezed the trigger of her assault rifle in a death spasm, but Holly had already moved out of harm's way.

"Agatha Raisin, you beauty," Holly said, looking down at the amateur sleuth novel in her hand.

A sound like 'nnnngghhh' came from behind her. She turned around and discovered they hadn't escaped unscathed after all.

"I think I'm dying. Not going to make it. You just... go on without me..." Rob said, his voice strained. Holly looked down at his hand, which was the only part of him that showed any sign of damage.

"Bad luck. You've lost a finger. It's hardly fatal though." She pulled him to his feet using the other hand.

"You don't know that! It could go septic. Or perhaps the smell of blood will attract a pack of wolves. They have wolves in Scotland, right?" he said, his eyes fixed on the stump where his middle finger once was.

Holly almost felt sorry for him. That was probably half of all the sign language he knew gone forever.

"Let's get out of here," she said, not wanting to look down at the bodies in the snow, or even think about the events of the weekend. How could anyone take such pleasure from the demise of people who - despite knowing for a deceptive reason - they'd associated with for years? If you were going to do away with a whole group, something like a bomb disguised as a gas leak would have been a far more efficient way to go.

Holly shook her head, wondering if she was starting to go loopy thinking about the best way to kill people. It was just that she couldn't comprehend the amount of hate you needed to have in order to plan each individual death in such a way that mocked their greatest cases.

"Crazy, so crazy," Rob said, trailing along next to her, but sticking to the footprints Tom had made (just in case).

"How could one person be so cruel?" Holly agreed, assuming he was following her thoughts.

"Yeah, that chocolate cake has gone to waste. All because she pretended it was poisoned! That's one less cake I'll be able to eat in my lifetime. It's just tragic," Rob said, and she thought he might even be tearing up a little. Holly decided to put it down to him being slightly delirious from the blood-loss and shock.

They followed Tom's last steps across a couple of fields to

the side of the main road, where he'd parked a surveillance van. Holly thought about trying the backdoor to see if it was open and taking a look inside, but then realised she didn't want to. It was from here that Tom had executed a group of people who'd thought he was their friend, just by pushing a few buttons.

The police could deal with it.

They trudged along the icy roads, trying not to slip over, both keeping their silence. It was a lengthy walk back to civilisation, and Holly somehow knew it would be a long time before they had a moment to themselves again. Also, her phone was out of battery. Rob hadn't even brought his with him on the trip, having presumably not expected any bad weather... or massacres.

She looked around at the winter trees in the gently fading light as the sun started to dip in the sky. They looked just as peaceful and unmoved as when she'd arrived at Horn Hill House. Yet, beneath their branches, the world had changed. Seven had lost their lives, and there would be no future mysteries solved by those six great minds. She'd like to think that there would be no great crimes committed either, but something told her that there would always be someone ready to take Miranda's place.

It was good of Rob to wait until they entered the foyer of the hospital to pass out. Carrying him would have been impossible. It was not as considerate that he stayed unconscious for an hour afterwards, leaving Holly to explain everything to the police.

By the time Rob came round and demanded food, the police had arrived at Horn Hill House and confirmed all that Holly had told them. The only thing she didn't like was the way the two police officers in the hospital room with her and Rob kept reaching down and touching their handcuffs.

Holly chewed her lip, remembering for the first time that she had technically killed someone. The weapon hadn't been hers, but she'd still ended a life. Would she get in trouble for it?

The strange thing was, the more Holly thought about it, the more she realised she didn't feel any remorse. Instead, there was an emptiness inside. The voice inside her head reminded her that Miranda had absolutely deserved it. If she'd done nothing, both she and Rob would be dead. Thinking practically about the matter was the only way to go. Not to mention, she'd probably done the police a big favour by eliminating one of the most successful criminals around. One they hadn't even known existed.

It wasn't long before the investigation uncovered the traps and found the van to be entirely clean of Rob and Holly's fingerprints or DNA. They were in the clear and hailed as heroes. The press arrived and took pictures and statements, and the rest of the night passed in a whirl. Holly didn't even have a moment to think about any repercussions she may be in danger of incurring - having very publicly ended Miranda's vast crime enterprise.

Saying goodbye was harder than expected.

Rob's hand was still wrapped in bandages when he hugged her goodbye. Holly had been going for a handshake, but Rob had surprised her. She'd returned the hug and had discovered that you didn't go through a deadly experience like the serial killings at Horn Hill House without forming a bond. This wasn't like the initial attraction that had existed between them when they'd first met, what now felt like an age ago. This was something deeper. Holly supposed it was the first spark of a real friendship.

"You shouldn't let an experience like this one put you off. I know it was a tough case, but we got the bad guys and got out alive. That's what matters," Rob had offered, just before they'd parted ways. Holly had smiled and nodded. On the inside, she'd been wondering what would have happened to her if she'd been the unlucky one and had lost a finger. That would have been the end of her piano career - and how else was she going to earn her crust? She'd put that to Rob and he'd immediately suggested that she become a professional private detective and forget all about musical tomfoolery.

He'd also pointed out that there was rather a shortage of them at the moment.

Holly smiled as she drove back towards Sussex, marvelling at the way the weather was cold, but much less bitter, the further down the country you went. There was no sign of any snowfall.

She idly wondered what her area of speciality would be if she did take the pathway of being a detective. Looking back at her previous cases, she'd either be looking at lost and found, or solving mass murders. Neither seemed very appealing.

Rob had offered to help her, should she decide that she wanted to go into business. He'd even hinted at partnering up for a few cases. He'd said that her observational skills and quick thinking had impressed him. She suspected that it was just his way of saying thanks for saving his life using a rather dangerous piece of popular literature.

Holly glanced down at a copy of the book she'd used to save her life. It had felt right to find a normal edition and actually read the novel.

She had to say, she was disappointed. The plot had been a perfect combination of twists and turns, but she'd already managed to figure out who the killer was, and she was only halfway through. If only things were that simple in real life. Looking back, there'd been next to no convenient clues to help them figure it out before the clock had gone down to zero. It really wasn't fair.

Another item was also on the front seat, hidden beneath the book. Her copy of one of the big broadsheets had her picture, blown up to a ridiculous size, on page two.

It was typical that her one shot at fame was a terrible one. Her hair was a winter-weather fright, and she had bags beneath her eyes from the lack of sleep the night before at Horn Hill House. It was definitely not one to frame and put on the wall. Somehow, Rob had contrived to look great - despite being in a hospital bed and wearing a usually unflattering hospital gown. Life was definitely not fair.

Holly shook her head as she neared Little Wemley. Things would be back to normal in no time. In a couple of weeks, this story would be forgotten. Holly would have returned to working as a professional pianist, putting her silly detective dreams behind her once and for all.

Deep in the glove compartment her phone began to ring. Holly ignored it and kept driving. The phone went dead, but after a moment's silence, it began to ring again. This time, she pulled over and answered.

"Hello?" she said, wondering if it was the police looking for more answers. She thought she'd finished with all that.

"Hello, Holly Winter? I've got a serious problem I think you may be able to help with. We suspect that my family's most prized heirloom, the Enviable Emerald, is under threat from thieves. We've informed the police, of course, but they say there's nothing they can do if a crime hasn't yet been committed. We desperately need the help of a private detective. I'm hoping you can solve the case before the crime even takes place," the man on the other end of the phone said.

Holly's immediate instinct was that it was all a prank. Her second was to put the phone down. Hadn't she just said that she was absolutely not going to be sucked into the world of private investigating?

"We'll compensate you generously for your time. How does..." He said a number so large it made Holly's mouth drop open a little. "...sound to you?"

It was more than she'd make working for two months as a pianist - and that was with a full performance schedule!

"You could stay in the house while you work on the case. I read all about your work up at Horn Hill House. I'm sure you can help us," the man pressed.

Holly found herself wavering.

What was one little case involving a not-even-stolen emerald? She'd take the money and the case, and then that would be it. She would settle down again to her nice normal life in Little Wemley. No more Nancy Drew or Agatha Raisin delusions.

Deep inside, she could already feel an itch of excitement as she contemplated the case she'd just accepted. Would she be able to find the thieves before they struck? Was there even a real threat to the emerald?

This is your last adventure, she promised herself.

READ ON FOR THE FIRST TWO
CHAPTERS OF A FATAL FROST!

A FATAL FROST

THE ENVIABLE EMERALD

Holly looked out of the window of her rented cottage. A thick frost covered the field that her property backed onto. She felt a little sorry for the smattering of wild deer she could see, whose coats also glistened with frost in the first rays of sunshine.

She stirred her breakfast hot chocolate - while she watched the deer graze on anything that wasn't frozen solid - and thought about everything she had to do.

Christmas was fast approaching. She'd almost entirely filled up her diary with piano bookings. From pantomimes to office parties, she was going to be very busy during the winter evenings.

Unusually for Holly, her days were pretty busy, too.

On her way back from the horrid happenings at Horn Hill House - where six of the country's greatest detectives had been murdered - she'd received a call about a case. After getting home and thinking it through a bit more, she'd officially accepted and had dashed straight off to assist the Uppington-Stanley family with the perceived threat to their Enviable Emerald.

Holly took another sip of her hot chocolate, made with real dark Belgian chocolate. There really was no better way to start the day, and being single, there was no one to judge her for it either.

She sat down at her kitchen table and flipped her laptop open. After the drama at Horn Hill House, she'd decided it was high time she familiarised herself with a little more technology. In order to get to grips with it, she'd started a blog about the smattering of past mysteries she had solved.

She told herself firmly that it was just so she'd have a way of looking back and remembering why it was such a bad and dangerous idea to become a private detective. However, the annoying little voice in her head whispered that having a blog would also be an excellent way for any potential clients to find out about her. Not to mention, it was fun writing the little stories. She only hoped that recounting them in third person wouldn't be considered big-headed. All of her favourite mysteries were written that way, and she also thought there was no harm in pretending she had a very astute assistant - as opposed to being a one-woman band.

"No more mysteries, remember?" Holly chided herself out loud, realising she was making grandiose plans for the future again. She opened up *The Case of the Enviable Emerald* and started to edit the beginning of the tale.

The problem was, even with all of the resolve in the world, mysteries had a habit of finding her. The simple case of the Enviable Emerald had been no exception when an unexpected complication had transformed it into a full-blown mystery.

Holly sighed a little as she stared at the text on the screen documenting her most recent adventure. *Your final adventure,* she reminded herself for the hundredth time. She copied and pasted it into a new post, clicked on 'preview', and began her final read-through.

The Case of the Enviable Emerald
A Holly Winter Mystery

The first mystery to solve in the case of the Enviable Emerald was why did the Uppington-Stanley family believe their priceless heirloom was under threat? It was unusual for a thief to be considerate enough to give their targets a handy heads-up. Uncovering the truth about why the family even suspected an attempt was imminent was the first thing Holly planned to do upon her arrival at Enviable Manor.

Enviable Manor was every bit as grand as it sounded. The walls had been crafted from grey sandstone, and the building had softened and weathered throughout the centuries. It still retained its original magnificence - the sign of a splendid architect.

After parking her car (which had been complaining ever since it had been left out in a Scottish blizzard) she walked up to the manor and rapped on the door, using the curiously elephant-shaped knocker - its trunk the moveable piece. A maid opened the door and she was invited in for afternoon tea with the Uppington-Stanleys. Despite being pleased by her timing and more pleased by the scones, cream, jam, and teas that were served, Holly knew that her burning question couldn't wait. Therefore, she only allowed herself a conservative three scones, piled high with mounds of cream and jam, before she asked why the Uppington-Stanleys thought that a theft was imminent.

It transpired that the wealthy family had visited their local Christmas fair, taking their children - Isabelle and Nick - with them. Both 'children' were in their twenties and had decided to visit the fortuneteller, who'd set up between the church's booze tombola and the Brownies' sweet stall. Holly had privately wondered about the wisdom of this stall placement on the part of the fair organisers.

The junior Uppington-Stanleys had entered the fortuneteller's tent, one after the other, and had both received the same warning: Your family's most prized heirloom is under threat. Defend your inheritance, or all will be lost, and you will suffer from misfortune forever.

"We found this a bit disconcerting," Mr Uppington-Stanley said, his eyebrows twitching up and down as he alternated between dismay and forced politeness at the number of scones the hired detective had managed to put away.

"Yes, it seemed awfully specific. We're sensible folk and don't believe in any claptrap fortune-telling nonsense, but this seemed like a genuine threat. After our children told us what they'd heard, we tried to find the fortuneteller, but she'd already gone, and the fair organisers had no contact details for her." Mrs Uppington-Stanley wrung her hands - most likely because of her fears about the emerald, but also possibly because Holly had started on the fairy cakes, and they were disappearing at an alarming rate.

"But if the fortuneteller was involved with jewel robbers, how does it benefit her to pre-warn her targets?" Holly mused.

The married couple shook their heads and tried not to look at the crumbs, which were all that remained of their afternoon tea.

"We're baffled by it. Either the woman knew something and perhaps wanted to warn us as a way of getting back at a person who had done her wrong, or she could be a complete crank who just happened to know about the family jewels.

They're quite famous," Mr Uppington-Stanley said with a completely straight face.

Holly tried not to choke on her final fairy cake.

"Well, you seem to have thought about the options," Holly observed, wondering what, exactly, they wanted her to do. Her lips twisted as she inwardly wrestled with the large figure the family had agreed to pay her for the job she was supposed to be doing and the simplicity of the task at hand.

"I should probably come up and have a look at the emerald and review your security measures. Then I'll be able to deduce if there could be any risk of theft," she said, not sure what else she was supposed to do.

The wealthy pair nodded agreeably.

Mrs Uppington-Stanley led her upstairs. They walked down a lengthy corridor, luxuriously carpeted with light-cream pile, the dark wood panels on the walls adding to the air of expense. Holly immediately felt guilty for keeping her shoes on.

"Here we are!" her guide announced, knocking on a panelled door that almost looked like part of the wall. Holly noted that it would be difficult for a casual thief to find the location of the emerald. They'd have to be an insider. Her employer pointed to a CCTV camera that had its lens permanently focused on the door - another security measure.

"Hello Mrs Uppington-Stanley," a man said, unlocking the door from the inside and letting the pair in.

"This is our full-time security guard, Nick. He stays in the room all day everyday, until he swaps with Lewis, our night watchman. Nick never leaves this room," Mrs Uppinton-Stanley announced, rather proudly.

Holly looked around the room and nodded vaguely. To her, the idea of employing a full-time security guard just to look after one jewel equated to some serious overkill, but she supposed if you had enough money, and possessed something as valuable and irreplaceable as the Enviable Emerald, it might be worth it.

"I have to admit, it seems as though you have the situation under control," Holly said, looking around the box room, which didn't even have a window. She hoped Nick was being well-compensated for what must be a very boring job.

"Yes, well… we thought it best to check," Mrs Uppington-Stanley said, slightly flushed from Holly's professional approval.

Holly tried not to feel like a complete fraud. She'd only really solved a couple of small cases and had barely managed to escape with her life from the Horn Hill House incident. That didn't really qualify her for professional consulting, but the Uppington-Stanley's offer had been so tempting…

"I'd better show you the emerald while we're up here. Just in case there is something we might have forgotten," Mrs Uppington-Stanley said, opening the drawer by the bed and pulling out a generic looking jewellery box covered in faded, dark-pink suede. The only thing that stood out about it was the rather flimsy lock, which was broken and hanging off at an angle.

Holly was about to ask if it was supposed to look damaged - as a sort of red herring - when Mrs Uppinton-Stanley's hands fumbled with the lid and flipped open the tall case to reveal… nothing at all.

The emerald was gone.

"No… NO! It can't be!" Mrs Uppington-Stanley wailed.

Holly heard the sound of running footsteps and Mr Uppington-Stanley appeared, his face morphing into a mask of horror when he heard the news.

"Tell me quickly, when was the last time you saw the emerald?" Holly asked, hoping the pair wouldn't dissolve into hysteria. It seemed to her that if the crime had only just been committed, there was a chance that the thief could still be apprehended.

"This morning. I took it out to show it to a visiting colonel over breakfast, but I put it straight back in its case and locked it with this key," Mrs Uppington-Stanley held up the dainty key. "You saw me do it, didn't you, Nick?"

The big security guard nodded. His, dark, expressionless face looked untroubled by the news. Holly supposed it was a professional requirement that he stayed calm in a crisis. She herself felt anything but calm. The gears in her head were already spinning as she felt time - and the emerald - slipping away from her.

"Let us assume the jewel was returned safely to the jewellery box. After all, the lock has been smashed, which implies that the emerald was taken from the drawer. Has anyone else but Nick been in this room since this morning? Anyone else at all?" she asked.

The Uppington-Stanleys shook their heads and then stopped and exchanged a glance.

"Only the maid, but she is watched by Nick. Nick himself hasn't left the room. Well, apart from attending to calls of nature. Even that facility is actually still in this room," Mr Uppington-Stanley explained, pointing to a small corner, which had been partitioned off and presumably contained a toilet.

"Is the maid still here at the manor? It's important that we speak to her if she and Nick were the only ones with access to the room."

Mrs Uppington-Stanley flapped her hands uselessly for a few more seconds and then trotted off, hopefully to find the maid.

Holly could have sworn that Mr Uppington-Stanley shot her a grateful look.

"Did you go to the bathroom while the maid was in here?"

she asked the security guard. He nodded, a little mournfully. Holly chewed her lip, looking again at the broken lock. Despite not being a very convincing lock, smashing it violently would have made some noise. She doubted that it could have been done without Nick hearing it.

"I was only in there for a couple of minutes. The maid was still cleaning when I came out. I know she hadn't left the room because I lock the door after everyone who comes in," Nick explained.

Holly looked pointedly at the currently open door. The guard shrugged. "Everyone apart from my employers, of course," he explained, like she was an idiot.

"What about this door?" Holly asked, noticing a rather ordinary looking cream door set in the wall by the sofa.

"It's always kept locked. I'm the only one with the key," Mr Uppington-Stanley patiently explained.

Holly looked it up and down and noticed that the bottom of the door was nearly flush to the bare-wood floor. "How big is the emerald?"

Mr Uppington-Stanley put his first fingertip against the tip of his thumb, forming a circle. Holly dismissed the possibility that it could have been passed under the door.

"Excuse me? What is the matter?" A young, dark-haired woman, with a surprisingly clipped British accent, entered the room, followed by a still-distraught Mrs Uppington-Stanley.

"You're the maid who cleaned this room earlier today?" Holly asked. The young woman nodded to confirm. She still held her basket of cleaning supplies, presumably from the job she had still been doing.

"May I?" Holly asked as a courtesy and quickly glanced through the supply bucket.

Nick shook his head. "It can't be in there. She doesn't bring much into the room. She just hoovers and dusts and listens to her music the whole time. The hoover is a little handheld thing that's entirely see-through. It wasn't even being used while I was in the toilet. Also, I search her when she leaves," he said, still sounding like he was explaining this to a person who was short of brain cells.

Holly tried not to be goaded... but failed. "From the evidence I've been presented with, I think it's obvious that one of you committed - or at least aided in - the theft of the emerald. The question is, which one of you was it, and where is the emerald now? Until I know that, no one must leave this house," she said, putting her foot down.

"Have you got any leads?" Mrs Uppington-Stanley asked, her expression in danger of dissolving into tears at any second. Holly suspected it was only the time it took to apply her artful makeup that was making her think twice about it.

Holly tried to nod more confidently than she felt. "I need to make a call," she said, praying that her hunch turned out to be right.

She'd only just finished the call when she heard a shout and raced back along the hall to the box room. Mr Uppington-Stanley stood with the Enviable Emerald in his hand. A small carry case, that must have belonged to the security guard, was open on the floor. Globs of hair gel splattered the floorboards and the surface of the emerald.

"Mystery solved! I think it's time we called the police. Our security guard is a jewel thief!" Mr Uppington-Stanley announced, his eyebrows knitted together in fury. "The butler and the chef are keeping a close eye on him. That slippery man! He had such good references, too," he added with a sigh, the fury being replaced with disappointment. "I suppose the temptation just got too much."

Holly chewed her lip again, the gears in her head still turning. "It is time to call the police, but I'm not sure that the case has been solved. Will you allow me to continue my investigation until they arrive?"

Mr Uppington-Stanley nodded, his eyes fixed on the emerald. "Feel free. The emerald is back, and that's what matters," he said and then walked out of the room, already shouting to the butler and chef to make sure Nick didn't try anything.

Holly was left in the empty box room with the strong feeling that she was missing something big. The phone call had been enough for her to figure out how the jewel was stolen, but she couldn't work out how it had left the room. Her eyes were drawn once more to the door leading into the spare room and she began to wonder...

"I've got it!" Holly announced, arriving back in the main room, her face flushed with pleasure. Everyone turned to look at her. She realised that Nick was already in handcuffs, the newly-arrived police having made the arrest immediately.

"We'll hear about it later. We have the emerald," Mr Uppington-Stanley said, dismissing her, as he gestured to the police to take Nick away.

Holly felt her temper rise. Why hire her if they didn't want her opinion? "That would be a mistake," she tried again. Mr Uppington-Stanley shot her a look of exasperation, but Holly hadn't finished. "That emerald is a fake," she announced, praying that she was correct. She hadn't had time to test her theory, as she'd heard the police turn up and had known that time had run out.

"If you'll follow me up to the room where the jewel was kept, I think I can solve this mystery. Oh, and everyone should come," she added.

Oh please, please be right about this! Holly thought, as she led the odd group up the stairs, down the corridor, and into the spare room next to the box room where the emerald had been kept.

"We're not in the right room," Mr Uppington-Stanley informed her, sounding deeply unimpressed. Holly ignored her wealthy employer and instead moved to the centre of the room, taking a deep breath.

It was time to *Miss Marple* this mystery.

"The first problem with this case was 'how?' How was it that the lock could be broken on the jewellery case without Nick the security guard hearing it? The obvious answer was that he did it himself when he was in the room unattended. I thought that was the most probable solution, until I noticed something in the maid's bucket. A lot of people listen to music when they clean, and I could see she had a music player of some sort, but there was something off about it. It looked like it had a kind of external speaker - something which MP3 players don't tend to have."

Holly paused and thanked her lucky stars that she'd done some Googling of the latest technology before she'd rushed off to the emerald case. Her lack of knowledge had let her down at Horn Hill House, but her research had paid off this time.

"It just so happens, that I recently read an article about some new technology. It's meant to still be theoretical, but I think it might have been used here. There is a device which can cancel out external noises by mimicking their frequencies and, therefore, eliminating them. The same applies to internal noises. This theoretical device could be used to create a personal bubble of silence, making it impossible for someone - even if they were very close by - to hear something like... a lock being smashed off a jewellery case," Holly finished. She looked up at her listeners and was met with a bunch of frowns.

"What?" one of the police officers asked, looking completely bamboozled.

Holly resisted the temptation to sigh. "I made a call to a friend who then called on a contact who works for the Ministry Of Defence. They confirmed that the silencing technology does actually exist, it's just not widely marketed yet. You'd have to be a specialist to get hold of it." Holly's eyes fell on the dark-haired maid. "How long have you worked here?"

The maid made a noise of derision. "You're really accusing me of this? The emerald was found in his hair gel!" she complained, and various voices around the room seemed to agree with her.

Holly looked at the bucket she was still holding and frowned. "Where's your MP3 player?"

The maid frowned right back. "It's right here," she said, pulling her phone from her pocket. Holly rubbed her temples. *Great.* The girl had managed to hide the device she'd seen, probably whilst waiting downstairs.

"This detective you've hired is crazy," the accused said, shaking her head.

The police began to move towards the door, taking Nick with them. Holly momentarily reflected that this kind of stuff never happened to Miss Marple. She'd better get on with the big reveal.

Well... what she hoped would be the big reveal.

"I realised that it wasn't possible to get the emerald out of the room through the door, as Nick would have found it when he searched the maid. We also know that he hadn't left the room all day, because you have CCTV outside the door. So, how did the emerald leave the room when there were no windows and doors for it to get through?" Holly asked the audience, but none of them was in the mood for joining in. She ignored their mutterings and bent down on one knee, running her hands over the floorboards by the door, trying to ignore the bead of sweat sliding down her spine. Was she about to make a huge fool of herself?

"Ah-ha!" she cried when her hand detected a loose board. She levered it up and discovered it slid completely out from under the door, leaving a handy hidey-hole that went from one room to the next. The removal of the board also revealed the real Enviable Emerald, glimmering in the dim light. Holly picked it up and held the remarkable jewel in the palm of her hand for all to see. She'd half-expected spontaneous applause, but there were only more surprised mutterings.

"Well, how do we know who committed the crime now, and how do we know which emerald is real?" the very annoying DCI said.

Holly tried not to grind her teeth in frustration. "If you go back downstairs and search the living room, I'm sure you'll find the noise blocker that I was talking about. It should have enough fingerprints on it to close the case. Also, maybe you could run a search or two and find out who our maid here really is. That sort of technology and this kind of crime... it's not the first jewel she's stolen, that's for sure."

"Yes, but, the emerald..." Mr Uppington-Stanley cut in, looking anxiously from one identical gem to the other.

Holly had to keep her cool once more. They never wrote about all of this stubborn idiocy in the detective stories she read! Everyone was always suitably in awe of the detective's brilliance.

"Obviously you wouldn't go to all the trouble to hide a fake jewel under the floorboards where no one is going to look! The fake jewel was planted where you'd be most likely to search, in order to frame Nick," she explained.

"But, the maid..." the policeman jumped in again, and Holly only just managed to stop herself from tearing her hair out.

"Do some research! Find out if she's been caught before. You'd better check the emerald as well for prints. Although, I, ah… touched it a bit," she said, realising she'd made what had to be a very amateur error. "When you take the jewels to a jeweller, you'll see," she finished, hoping they'd finished their cross examination.

"That doesn't explain the fortuneteller, though…" Mrs Uppington-Stanley jumped in.

Holly bit her lip. That was one mystery she hadn't solved.

"Who knows, perhaps she got lucky?" she offered.

"Well, I suppose that's that then," Mr Uppington-Stanley concluded.

The End.

Holly's brow creased when she read the last couple of lines of her story. The ending was definitely a bit of a let down, but then, that's what had really happened.

The police had carted off both suspects for questioning because they'd had no faith in Holly's investigation. One of the officers had even had the cheek to imply that she might have planned the whole thing herself! Fortunately, he'd stopped talking when someone had whispered in his ear that she'd been a part of the Horn Hill House massacre. By default, the officer must have assumed she was a great detective - the same way her first proper employers had.

She'd later been informed that the maid did have a criminal record. Further investigation had turned up her involvement in a number of high profile jewel thefts. Nick the security guard was released, and the maid was going be tried and sentenced for her attempted crime, and anything else the police could find and get to stick…

Holly drained the last few dregs of her hot chocolate and

thought about the cheque that had been couriered to her the day after she'd finished her investigation. That was something at least. She wondered what she'd do with the money. It meant she didn't need to accept as many Christmas piano gigs.

She'd started the season with the intention of turning down any booking that didn't sound like it would be a good show, but the more she'd said no, the more people had asked. Ironically, people thinking she was in demand had actually made her far more popular. She smiled a little. She didn't mind in the slightest.

She was one of those lucky few people who thoroughly enjoy what they do to make a living. Playing piano was a true passion. She'd worked for many years to reach a very high standard, and she still longed to be better. There was always room for improvement.

Her fingers spasmed indecisively for a moment, before she reached for her mobile phone, reluctantly searching through her address book. She dialled the number. It was answered after just two rings.

"I knew you'd come around." Rob Frost's voice floated back down the line to her, with more than a hint of a gloat in it.

Holly bit her lip.

"Wait... that is why you called right? You have changed your mind?" Rob tried to clarify, ruining his cool-guy first line.

Holly smirked. "I think so. I was reading back through the Enviable Emerald case and... it wasn't so bad. Nobody died, and the mystery got solved. So, I was thinking, if I could just have a few more cases like that one... it wouldn't be too dangerous. It should just be fun, right?" she said, and could almost hear Rob's smile of triumph.

"You've got the mystery-solving bug. I knew you wouldn't

quit on me! Now, about the profitable enterprise we're poised to enter into..." He started to reel off a long list of things that Holly would need to do in order to set up her very own private detective business, endorsed by Rob Frost - the great private detective.

Amazingly, Rob hadn't wanted any money for his endorsement. He was doing it all as a favour in return for the time that Holly had saved his life using a rather deadly amateur detective novel.

At least... she was pretty sure that was why he was helping her.

Holly shook her head and took some more notes.

Rob was based in Cornwall at the moment, searching for... something. He'd been vague about the details of the case he was supposedly working on. It meant that he wasn't going to be popping by for tea anytime soon. Any romantic notions Holly might have had were quashed.

"Just remember, you're using my name in your business, so don't screw it up!" Rob warned, but Holly knew he was grinning that beautiful smile of his. His dark hair was probably all mussed up as well, and...

She stopped herself right there.

"I'll do my best. You'd better not do anything stupid either. We're tied together now," she said and immediately bit her tongue.

Rob laughed. "Talk to you soon, Holly."

Holly stared at the mobile phone and sighed. Things had been so intense during the short time she'd spent at Horn Hill House, she hadn't really had a chance to figure out how she felt about Rob. After they'd survived the ordeal and had dealt with the press together, there'd been a seed of friendship between them, which had grown into this business venture that Rob had practically pressured her into. Holly bit back a smile. She hadn't needed much persuading.

She'd sworn off mysteries after Horn Hill House, but the recent case of the Enviable Emerald had reminded her that solving mysteries didn't have to be a terrifying pastime - and she was actually really good at it! Her vast knowledge of mystery books and their story-lines meant she was expecting most twists and turns and could always crack the case.

This detective business wasn't going to be serious anyway. She'd just pick up a few little mysteries, perhaps focusing on lost and found type cases, and the kind of thing that came up locally. Definitely no big crime and absolutely no murders.

What could go wrong?

THE NO.1 LADIES' DETECTIVE AGENCY

"**I**'ve rented a little office space, put up a sign, and placed adverts in the local paper and around town. I've designed a website and added the blog to it, so people can read all about the cases and find us online. I've even started a social media page," she said into the phone.

Her eyes flicked back to the Facebook page with its seriously unflattering profile picture of her. The only picture she had in any professional capacity was the one that had been taken by the press after the Horn Hill House massacre. Her hair was a horror wig, and walking miles in freezing temperatures - trying not to get blown up by landmines - had done nothing for her skin. She sighed and promised herself she'd solve another case soon - and this time it would be a far more glamorous occasion when the press arrived.

"Cool, I like Facebook! I shall like your page..." Rob said on the other end of the phone.

As Holly watched the screen, her little 'like' counter jumped from two to three. Rob had liked it, she'd liked it, and her sister had liked it, too. Although, knowing her sister, it was probably so she could see if the business failed.

"Well, it's a start," Holly said, trying not to sound as unsure as she felt. "What should I do next?"

There was an awkward pause.

"Good question. I've never actually set up an agency before," Rob admitted.

Holly felt her stomach drop. "What?!"

She'd assumed that Rob had known what he was talking about, having got years of experience and successful cases under his belt.

"Mostly, I don't get given cases. I just… sort of stumble upon them," Rob admitted, and while Holly desperately wanted to ask exactly what he meant by that, now wasn't the time.

"So, I'm just your little experiment, am I?" Holly asked, feeling crosser by the second. This was so typical of Rob.

"Hey, I'm funding this too," he reminded her. "We're both taking a risk." There was a pause. "I don't know… when I look at you, I just think of how perfect you'd be working as a detective in a little town… solving all of the missing cat cases."

"Now you're just being a jerk," she told him.

Rob had the audacity to laugh. "Come on, lost cats make super hard cases! You can never predict what the little psychos will do next, which makes them hard to locate. I swear I wasn't making fun… or even kidding. Most of your cases will probably be lost cats," he said, his apology vanishing.

Holly would have loved to be able to correct him, but the two cases she'd previously worked on in Little Wemley had involved a lost dog and the mayor's chain - which had been stolen by the world's worst thief and recovered almost immediately. Rob's prediction was probably correct.

"What am I supposed to do? Just sit here and wait for the phone to ring?" Holly griped.

Rob was about to answer when the landline started to ring. Holly heard a snicker of amusement right before Rob put the phone down.

The landline continued to ring. She stared at it for a couple more rings, before finally lifting up the receiver.

"Hello, Holly Winter speaking," she said and heard a rather surprised noise on the other end of the phone.

"Oh, good. You're who I wanted to speak to. I found your details online, and I wanted to invite you to an event I'm putting on. It's a murder mystery night re-enactment of what happened at Horn Hill House. It would be just brilliant if you could appear at the end and answer any questions our pretend detectives might have. It's a charity event, so I'm afraid there's no budget available for…"

Holly put the phone down and shook her head in disbelief. How could anyone be dense enough to think that she'd want to be a part of some twisted re-enactment? That misguided organiser was giving the world of mystery-solving a bad name.

She snorted when she recalled the last line about a lack of budget. She'd heard that old chestnut a fair few times. It was always the same with 'charity events'. There was never any budget for the entertainment, but you knew that the bar would still be selling their drinks at a profit, and that pretty much everyone else at the event would still be getting paid.

Holly sighed. She had nothing against charity - she even occasionally agree to take part in genuine charity events - but what had just been proposed to her on the phone was ludicrous and offensive.

She frowned for a second and then decisively opened a Word document. Now that her agency was starting to become more visible, (although how, she wasn't really sure) she would need to hire someone to deal with answering the phone. The only problem was, she didn't have a huge budget herself. Holly ran her hands through her hair, well aware that she was dangerously close to becoming as unreasonable as the charity events organiser. Perhaps she could take on an apprentice and pay them minimum wage, and only as a part-timer. She had a bit of leeway afforded by the cheque she'd received for solving the Enviable Emerald case. All she needed was a few more of those and she'd be in profit and able to pay a secretary. After a moment's further delibera-tion, she decided it was worth the risk. Someone else could deal with the cranks on the phone.

Ten minutes later, she was out pinning up her adverts around town and had asked the local paper to place a job available ad. Now all there was to do was wait.

And wait.

Holly sat in her office for the entire day and no one came in.

She knew that starting a business was never easy, and business was hard to come by until the word spread, but she'd still been hopeful. Perhaps she should ask Rob how he came by his cases and start doing whatever it was that he did. There had to be a way to make a name for herself! For now though, it was the end of an uneventful first day, and she had her resident gig at the Little Wemley Cocktail Bar to play that evening.

The next morning, Holly received a few phone calls, all asking about the job. She also had two 'business' phone calls that both turned out to be complete junk. One was a prank call and the other caller had wanted to interview her for his next true crime book - *The Massacre of Horn Hill House*. Holly had reiterated that she didn't want to talk about it. After a little more prying, it had also transpired that the 'writer' had never actually written a book before. Holly had put the phone down again and reflected that she really did need a good secretary to screen calls like this one.

Her first real job landed around lunchtime.

She received a call from a village local who suspected that someone had stolen her pearl necklace. Holly had popped around, and after a very brief investigation, she'd realised that the woman's Corgi had dragged the pearls out of the box and under the sofa. Fortunately, the corgi was so ancient it didn't have many teeth left, so the precious necklace was largely un-chewed. Holly hadn't had the heart to charge the woman anything like the minimum amount she and Rob had agreed was fair reimbursement for taking on a case, so she'd taken a nominal fee and left to get back to her little office, just in time for some late afternoon interviews.

She had three candidates lined up, but after looking at the CVs they'd sent through, she wasn't any closer to picking her secretary. With the low wage and hours available, Holly knew she could hardly afford to pick and choose.

The first candidate was still in school, which made her an impossible option, as Holly needed someone to work part-time in the day. The second was a little old lady, who wanted some easy work to make a little extra during her 'retirement'. Holly felt a bit sorry for her, and would have been tempted, as the woman had years of secretarial experience. The only problem was, she was incredibly hard of hearing and Holly knew she couldn't answer the phone. That just left her with the last option… and it wasn't a pleasant one.

Becky Stoney wasn't a secretarial dream come true. She had skin the colour of light coffee, thick, black hair she swept back into a bun, and a scowl that could make milk curdle at fifty-paces. At the start of the interview, Holly had immediately thought that Becky didn't like her. It was only later on that she'd discovered it wasn't anything personal - Becky didn't like anyone. But unfortunately, she wasn't still in school and she could hear perfectly well, which automatically made her the obvious choice for the job.

"Could you start on Monday?" Holly asked, half-hoping that Becky would be awkward about working, while her sensible side sternly reminded her that she needed an assistant - and with her budget, this was apparently as good as it got.

"Okay," Becky said and promptly left the office without a 'thanks' or a 'goodbye'.

I suppose it might show that she's efficient, Holly mused, but couldn't help wondering if she'd live to regret employing this cactus of a woman.

The next day and the weekend passed in a blur of little cases (several mislaid items and - you guessed it - lost cats) and piano performances. Holly was using all of her time when she wasn't solving cases to look through the endless sheets of Christmas piano music she had in her possession, poised to deal with just about any request that her many audiences might throw at her.

She was so engrossed in this practice, she'd forgotten all about Becky starting work on Monday. That was... until the woman herself stomped into the room, threw her ugly, black leather bag down in the middle of the floor, and plonked herself behind the other desk next to Holly.

"Oh! Good morning?" Holly ventured, and then bit her tongue when Becky just stared at her vacantly. Right on cue, the phone began to ring.

Her new secretary immediately seized it. "What do you want?" she demanded.

Holly winced. She could just about hear the caller on the other end of the line.

"Hello, er... is that Holly Winter I'm speaking to?"

Becky stared at the handset for a second before answering. "No," she replied and put the phone down.

Holly wondered if it was too late to call back the little old lady who was deaf as a post...

"I think we should discuss a phone answering protocol. Perhaps you could start by saying 'Hello, *Frost and Winter Detective Agency*. How may I help you?" she suggested.

Becky's eyes glazed over.

The phone began to ring again. This time, Holly made a grab for it. Becky reached at the same time. They were still playing tug-of-war with the handset when their first ever walk-in client entered the office.

"Good morning! I'm Holly Winter, head private detective at *Frost and Winter Detective Agency*," Holly felt compelled to add, in an attempt to hammer home her seniority to Becky.

Becky wasn't even looking her way. She was on the phone again, and from what Holly could overhear, things were heading in a similar direction to that of the last call. She slapped a smile on her face and properly focused on the visitor.

He was in his late twenties and possessed an unusual head of very pale blonde hair. The hair seemed a little out of place with his dark eyebrows, but Holly could tell he was all-natural, and his eyes were similarly dark. He was dressed in a tailored, navy-blue winter jacket, thrown on over suit-trousers and a shirt. All in all, he looked like he might have just stepped off the page of a magazine, rather than off the street in Little Wemley.

Holly tried to un-notice everything she'd just seen, but it was difficult to ignore the man's perfect appearance. Even Becky fluffed up her bun and did her best to sound as efficient at getting rid of people on the phone as she could.

"A private detective? I had no idea those things really existed outside of storybooks. What cases have you worked on?" the stranger asked. Holly felt her heart sink a little. Clearly, he wasn't here with a mystery for her.

"Oh, this and that," she said airily. "I recently recovered the Enviable Emerald when it was briefly stolen from the Uppington-Stanley family," she said.

The stranger's forehead developed a crease, while he studied her intensely. Holly hoped her cheeks weren't as pink as she suspected they were.

"Now I know where I've seen you before! You were in the papers during that Horn Hill disaster."

Holly decided not to correct him on his use of the word 'disaster'. A disaster usually signified an event that was unavoidable, and that no one could have predicted. The murders at Horn Hill House had been planned and executed with full knowledge and intention.

"Yes, I was. How may I help you today?" she asked, finding her smile again and trying to move the conversation away from the newspaper clipping and *that* photo.

Her visitor raised a hand to his head, showing his forgetfulness. "Wow, I haven't even introduced myself. I'm George Strauss, chairman of the Little Wemley Archaeological Society."

Holly raised an eyebrow. "I had no idea that there was a society of amateur archaeologists so close to Little Wemley."

Her visitor nodded, his enthusiasm overcoming any reservations Holly may have had. "Indeed. We generally meet to discuss any finds. We also talk about past events of historical interest and argue about what may, or may not, have occurred. The older the event and the evidence, the harder it is to be sure what really happened during that time - which is why it makes for such a compelling debate." He smiled and Holly found herself hopelessly smiling back at him.

"So, ah, Mr Strauss…"

"George," he corrected.

"What brings you to the agency?" she finally got round to asking.

George ruffled his pleasantly side-parted hair, clearly embarrassed to have been sidetracked. "Yes, of course! I'm looking for a pianist for the annual Christmas dinner of the Archaeological Society, and you were highly recommended. I called at the post office and they told me I could find you here," he said, probably over-explaining a little, so he didn't come across as a wandering weirdo.

"I'll just check my diary," she told him, feeling her heart sink further still. It wasn't that she wasn't happy to accept the piano booking, but an evening playing piano meant she wouldn't get to socialise at all with this handsome stranger. It would be one night of wistful longing, and then it would be over. Holly wished things could be different.

Had she known what was just around the corner, she wouldn't have made that wish.

BOOKS IN THE SERIES

Snowed in with Death

A Fatal Frost

Murder Beneath the Mistletoe

Winter's Last Victim

Prequel: The First Frost

A REVIEW IS WORTH ITS WEIGHT IN GOLD!

I really hope you enjoyed reading this story. I was wondering if you could spare a couple of moments to rate and review this book? As an indie author, one of the best ways you can help support my dream of being an author is to leave me a review on your favourite online book store, or even tell your friends.

Reviews help other readers, just like you, to take a chance on a new writer!

Thank you!
Ruby Loren

ALSO BY RUBY LOREN

MADIGAN AMOS ZOO MYSTERIES

Penguins and Mortal Peril

The Silence of the Snakes

Murder is a Monkey's Game

The Peacock's Poison

A Memory for Murder

Whales and a Watery Grave

Chameleons and a Corpse

Foxes and Fatal Attraction

Monday's Murderer

Prequel: Parrots and Payback

EMILY HAVERSSON OLD HOUSE MYSTERIES

The Lavender of Larch Hall

The Leaves of Llewellyn Keep

The Snow of Severly Castle

The Frost of Friston Manor

The Heart of Heathley House

JANUARY CHEVALIER SUPERNATURAL MYSTERIES

Death's Dark Horse

Death's Hexed Hobnobs

Death's Endless Enchanter

Death's Ethereal Enemy

Death's Last Laugh

Prequel: Death's Reckless Reaper

HAYLEY ARGENT HORSE MYSTERIES

The Swallow's Storm

The Starling's Summer

The Falcon's Frost

The Waxwing's Winter

BLOOMING SERIES

Blooming

Abscission

Frost-Bitten

Blossoming

Flowering

Fruition

Made in the USA
Monee, IL
20 September 2020

43052415R00069